For my mom, who supplied me with mountains of library books and let me read them in a tree. For hours.

SEPTEMBER SHADOWS

JUSTICE, MONTANA SERIES
- Book One -

DEBBI MIGIT

Scrivenings
PRESS
Quench your thirst for story.
www.ScriveningsPress.com

Published by Scrivenings Press LLC
15 Lucky Lane
Morrilton, Arkansas 72110
https://ScriveningsPress.com

Printed in the United States of America

Paperback ISBN 978-1-64917-086-6

eBook ISBN 978-1-64917-087-3

Library of Congress Control Number: 2020949288

Cover by www.bookmarketinggraphics.com.

Scripture quotations marked (NIV) are taken from the Holy Bible, New International Version®, NIV®. Copyright © 1973, 1978, 1984, 2011 by Biblica, Inc.™ Used by permission of Zondervan. All rights reserved.

Scripture quotations marked (NCV) are taken from the New Century Version®. Copyright © 2005 by Thomas Nelson, Inc. Used by permission. All rights reserved.

Scripture quotations marked (NLT) are taken from the Holy Bible, New Living Translation, copyright © 1996, 2004, 2007 by Tyndale House Foundation. Used by permission of Tyndale House Publishers, Inc., Carol Stream, IL 60188. All rights reserved.

All characters are fictional, and any resemblance to real people, either factional or historical, is purely coincidental.

ACKNOWLEDGMENTS

1. My husband, Phil, who delivered food to my desk when I was on a deadline and encouraged me in all things writerly.

2. My kids, who snuck in for hugs even when the door was closed.

3. Christine, Aunt Carol, Krista, and Leslie, who opened their homes (and cabin!) to me for personal writing retreats.

4. Jen Miller for her valuable insight and encouragement.

5. Linda Nixon Fulkerson and Shannon Taylor Vannatter at Scrivenings Press and Kathy Cretsinger at Mantle Rock Publishing. Thank you!

1

Saturday, September 1
1:00 p.m.

"Look out for that car!"

Horn blaring, I grip the steering wheel and jerk the truck into the right lane, narrowly avoiding a collision with a white Lucerne. The driver's face is as pale as her Buick, her mouth forming a tiny *O* as she gapes at me. Great. I almost took out sweet Mrs. Fairfax, the town librarian.

"Jess, stay in your lane. That car was in your blind spot."

I glare at Cole McBride. It's the same glare I used when we met on the playground during a four-square scuffle. I'd been the stubborn first-grader, and he was the determined third-grader. Not much has changed over the years. Well, we're taller.

"First, you told me to keep my eyes on the road. Then you said change lanes. I did that. And quit yelling at me!" I swing Cole's red Ford 150 pickup into Walmart's parking lot and turn off the engine.

The Saturday morning traffic rolls by as the residents of Justice, Montana, kick off their weekend errands.

A strand of hair escapes my braid, and I brush it aside,

waiting, as Cole tries to control his temper. I'm pretty sure I hear him counting to ten in Sioux, and the little vein in his neck stands out farther. That's not a good sign. Cole's easygoing, but sometimes I bring out the worst in him.

"I wasn't yelling," he says through gritted teeth. "You asked me to instruct you. I was instructing."

I grin. "You were instructing all right. At the top of your lungs. You can relax, Cole. I won't damage your truck."

When he bought the truck, it needed some work, but Cole fixed it up, and now it's his pride and joy. It shocked me when he offered to use it for my driving lessons.

"It's not the truck I'm worried about—I can fix it. But that car aimed right for you, and I don't think I can find replacement parts as easily."

Cole's tone and the warmth in his eyes make me catch my breath. Lately, our relationship seems to be changing. We're spending more time together as he teaches me to drive.

Something is shifting, which makes me both thrilled and terrified. Cole's my oldest friend, and I would never want that to change. But I can't deny I want more than friendship with him. And I suspect he feels the same way.

"C'mon. Give me the keys."

I wrap my smaller fingers around the set of keys. "No. Let me do it. The traffic confused me for a few minutes, but I'm fine now. Let's drive up Route 278, where it's not so crowded."

Cole raises a dark eyebrow and quirks his lips. "Yeah. Justice is a real metropolis. I'll bet we passed at least ten cars today."

"But I need to practice driving on the mountain roads, too, right?" My voice trails off as Cole shakes his head. I can hear Roxie, Cole's Australian Shepherd, pacing restlessly in the pickup bed. She doesn't enjoy long stops.

"Sorry, Jess. We need to check on Chieftain. Ben said he injured a fetlock yesterday, so I promised I'd keep an eye on him. Plus, I figured you'd be excited to start your new job."

Cole climbs out, his long strides taking him to the tailgate.

He lowers it, and Roxie leaps down, running to nudge me out of the driver's seat. I slide over to ride shotgun while Roxie, then Cole, squeeze into the cab.

"I'll bet Chieftain's not the only thing you'll be watching," I whisper out the window.

Amy Sinclair boards her horse, Damsel, at Hadley's ranch. Amy and Cole are seniors, and lately, she makes it a point to exercise Damsel whenever Cole works. As a member of the wealthiest family in Beaverhead County, Amy gets everything she wants. I just hope the one thing she can't have is Cole. She doesn't deserve him. I take a second to wonder if I feel protective or jealous. Probably both.

"Hey, don't sulk." Cole yanks the end of the braid hanging over my shoulder.

For a minute, I'm afraid I've expressed my opinion of Amy aloud, but then I realize he thinks I'm annoyed because he's taken the keys away from me. Sitting up straighter in the seat, I offer him a grin.

"That's okay. I know you're busy. Mark Crowley offered to take me driving sometime. I can call him." Did I really say that? What's going on with me, anyway?

Cole's dark eyebrows lower, and his grey eyes are nearly black as he scowls. "Mark Crowley is an idiot. He's already wrecked two cars, and he's barely seventeen. The last time Nick arrested him for drunk driving, and the only reason Mark didn't lose his license is because his dad's on the city council. Don't you even think of getting into his car!"

I consider this, then give a bright smile. "Don't worry, Cole. I'll drive."

Cole makes a growly noise, but he doesn't take the bait. Instead, he glances at the bag by my feet.

"You brought old clothes to change into, right?" He eyes my shredded jeans and green hoodie with concern.

"Oh yeah. I came prepared. I've seen you when you've

finished working at Hadley's. I brought the grungiest stuff I own."

"Great." He nods his approval. As we travel the five miles to the Hadley ranch, Cole explains my new duties. "You'll clean out stalls and maintain the equipment. Eventually, you'll help feed the horses."

"When can I exercise them?" I ask. Ben Hadley boards some of the finest horses in the county. I can't wait to ride them.

Cole turns the pickup off Route 278 and onto the dirt road that borders Rattlesnake Creek. Straight ahead is Hadley's Ranch and Stables. He drives under the wooden arch and down the unpaved road, his tires sending swirls of dust behind us.

"Well, Ben is cautious about who rides the horses." He pulls into the circular drive and parks the truck near the stables. "When he gets to know you, he'll see how mature and responsible you are. Exercise will come *much* later."

"Uh, I'm not sure how to take that." I climb down from the cab.

He grins. "C'mon. Grab your bag, and I'll show you where to change." He leads me through the stable yard and into a small equipment building. "There's a bathroom down the hall. When you're ready, come to the main stable next door, and we'll get to work." Then he's gone.

After I change into my old jeans and a T-shirt, I search for Cole. I find him in the paddock, brushing Chieftain. The magnificent black stallion belongs to Amy's uncle, Robert Sinclair, who's also my sister Sly's boss at Sinclair Construction. When Cole sees me, he gives a quick nod.

"You look good in grunge."

"Thanks." Compliments from Cole are rare. I duck my head, pleased.

He studies me for a minute. "Wait. This might help." He removes his baseball cap emblazoned with the Montana Grizzlies emblem and hands it to me.

I gather my long hair, tucking it under the rim, and settle the cap on my head.

Cole grins and tugs the bill down a little more securely. "Perfect."

Leading me to a vacant stall, he lays a tarp near the door. He hands me a pitchfork, showing me how to sift through the straw and toss the soiled part onto the tarp. Later, he'll put the tarp into the wheelbarrow for disposal.

The next hour is spent cleaning horse stalls. I'm deep in a fantasy of a hot bubble bath when a snicker sounds behind me. I turn around to see Amy Sinclair leaning against the side of the stall, watching me.

"Well, well, what have we here?" she sneers. "Hadley's has a new stable hand. Here boy, my mare's stall needs cleaned out next."

I glare at her and pull Cole's cap from my head, tumbling my dark hair around my shoulders.

"Why, if it isn't Jess Thomas!" Amy says in mock surprise. "I thought you were a boy Ben hired."

I figure I was grimy before, but now I feel completely filthy. Amy wears cream-colored jodhpurs, a sky-blue blouse, and shiny black boots, which I'm certain would show my reflection. Her white-blonde hair would never think of coming loose from her perfect French braid.

I draw a deep breath and mentally count to ten—in Gaelic. *Aon, dha, tri, ceitmy* ... Cole taught me a few Gaelic words and suggested counting in Gaelic might slow my temper quicker than in English since I have to concentrate harder.

When I reach *deich*, I say brightly, "No, Amy, it's me. Are you riding today?"

Her perfectly arched eyebrows raise a fraction. "No. I'm going dancing." Her tone drips with sarcasm. "I'm waiting for Cole. We're taking Damsel and Chieftain out for a while. We ride together every day, you know." She smirks.

I didn't, but I'd sooner be boiled in hot oil than admit it to Amy. I settle for giving her a slight, bored smile.

"How nice for you." I turn back to my work.

She views the pile of manure I'm shoveling and wrinkles her nose in disgust. "Don't forget to clean Damsel's stall while we're out," she orders. With one more sniff, she leaves.

I jam the pitchfork into the straw with a little more force than necessary. Cole has been busy grooming the horses over in the other stable ever since we started working. He didn't mention his riding date with Amy.

My feelings for Cole confuse me. He dated several girls throughout high school, and it didn't bother me ... much. But when my parents died, he was right there, holding me up— sometimes literally. Over time, our light-hearted and friendly conversations have deepened as we share our individual hopes and dreams for the future.

Now, I feel betrayed. I continue cleaning, my temper simmering over Amy's taunts. I toss a particularly disgusting piece of straw over my shoulder.

"Hey!" Cole's startled voice sounds behind me. "Be careful where you sling that stuff, Jess."

I swing around to see him brushing the sleeve of his denim jacket. His jeans are dusty, and his tousled black hair is messy, but it makes him look even more appealing. The jerk.

"Sorry," I say, insincerely.

Cole studies me through narrowed eyes. "Is something wrong? I warned you it's dirty work."

I turn away. "No. Nothing is wrong," I lie. "It will take me a few days to get used to it, that's all."

"Did you talk to Amy? Ben says she headed this way."

"Yes. She was here a minute ago." I scoop more straw over my shoulder. "She went looking for you." I turn and glare at him through the curtain of my hair.

"Okay. Jess, you can take a break if you're getting tired," he says, studying me with concern.

"I told you, I'm fine," I snap. "You'd better not be late for your date with The Princess."

He opens his mouth.

"Cole, let's go," Amy calls.

"I'll be right there, Amy." He glances over as she appears in the open doorway. "Why don't you lead Damsel around, and we'll leave in a second?"

Her mouth tightens, but after a moment, she moves away. "Hurry, please."

"Maybe you shouldn't have a weapon right now." Cole grins and takes the pitchfork, propping it against the stall.

I fold my arms across my chest. "You'd better go, Cole. You heard Amy. It wouldn't do to keep the Sinclair Princess waiting."

He frowns and reaches over, tipping my chin with his finger. Gazing into his eyes, I almost forget my anger. Who am I kidding—I almost forget my name.

"Jess—"

"I'm waiting," Amy shouts.

He gives an exasperated sigh. "We'll talk later." He turns and strides from the barn.

Frustration floods through me. It seems like Cole was ready to say something significant when Amy derailed him. "Must not have been too important if just a call from The Princess changed his mind," I grumble to myself. "We'll talk later," I mimic as I retrieve the pitchfork. "Who does he think he is? It doesn't matter to me what he does."

My hard work pays off, and by the time they return, the stable is gleaming. As Amy passes, she shoots me a gloating glance over her shoulder, and I regret there's no more disgusting straw in reach.

Five-thirty arrives, and we climb into Cole's truck for the trip home. He pulls onto the highway, then looks at me and sighs.

"Okay, Jess, I can see the steam rising. What did Amy say to you?"

I glare out of the side window and shrug. "I'm not sure what you mean."

He makes a sound of disgust. "Jess, she said something to make you mad. Earlier, when I stopped by, you were in a great mood. Even mucking out the stalls didn't seem to bother you. The next thing I know, Amy arrived, and you were dumping ... straw ... on me. Now, what happened?"

I realize I won't be able to distract him, so I might as well voice the turmoil that's been roiling in me all afternoon.

"Amy told me the two of you have a date every afternoon. Here I've imagined you working hard after school when in reality you've been riding with The Princess." My eyes flash with the accusation.

Cole's mouth tightens as he grips the steering wheel, then pulls off the highway. He parks in a scenic overlook that offers a fantastic view of Bannack State Park. Unfastening his seatbelt, he shifts closer to me. I move away, but he stops me by laying his hand on my arm.

"First, Jess, I don't go riding with Amy every afternoon. She's worried about Damsel's gait and asked me to check her. Chieftain needed exercise, so I told her I'd come along and see if there's a problem. Whatever she told you about any other rides isn't true. This is the first time we've ever ridden together."

"But she was practically all over you."

"I get that you don't care for her, Jess, but she isn't bad once you get to know her."

I roll my eyes.

He laughs. "Or maybe not. But Amy's a valuable customer of Hadley's, and I'm employed by them."

I stare out the window, determined to stay mad. Amy makes me feel like I'm only good for mucking the stables. Like I'm not good enough for Cole, and I worry she's right. It hurts, and for me, hurt sometimes looks like anger.

"Jess." Cole's tone sounds vulnerable.

I face him. His expression mixes frustration and concern

with something else. I wish I could define it. Whatever it is, I'm having trouble catching my breath.

"That's all it is, Jess. Work."

My anger forgotten, I tremble a little as he reaches to pull me closer. He leans down, and I close my eyes. Cole is going to kiss me, and I'm covered in horse yuck and straw.

Whoop, whoop.

We jump apart as if we've been scalded and see Nick McBride, Cole's older brother, drive by in a Sheriff's Department squad car. Deputy Nick laughs, shaking his finger at us. Cole waves back.

"Busted," he says, scooting across the seat and pulling the truck onto the highway.

I brush my hair away from my warm cheeks. "See what happens when you have a brother who's a cop," I grin. "You can't get away with anything."

A few minutes later, I breeze into my house and head for the shower. I replay our almost-kiss. At least, I believe Cole had been ready to kiss me. But what do I know? Lately, I've caught him looking at me like he's seeing me for the first time.

Several girls at school say Cole is hot. But it hasn't affected me, other than when they join us at the Dairy Barn, uninvited. Apparently, it doesn't occur to anyone I might be dating Cole. People are so used to seeing us together, they probably view us as brother and sister.

But I definitely don't think of him as a sibling, and I hope he doesn't see me that way either. My best friend, Grace Compton, recently said she noticed Cole studying me with a curious expression.

'It's like he's trying to memorize your face,' she said.

I'd blushed and laughed it off, but today has convinced me. I'm torn between seeing what develops between us and risking our deep friendship.

The past ten months have been the hardest of my life. On a November afternoon last year, my parents drove to Billings to

9

get my birthday present. I'd caught them smiling at me and whispering together for days, and I knew this would be a special gift.

It was snowing as they walked to the car that day. I'd laughed when I saw my dad scoop a little snow and touch the back of Mamma's neck. Shrieking in surprise, Mamma laughed and threw a handful of the cold stuff back at Dad. They climbed into the car, still laughing as they drove away. That is my last memory of my parents. An accident took them from me.

Those weeks are still a blur. My older sister, Sly, came home from college and became guardian of me and our younger sister, Maggie. But one thing remained constant. Cole. He held me when I cried, somehow realizing no words would be enough.

Now, thinking our relationship might go to a new level is equally thrilling and terrifying.

After my shower, I enter the empty kitchen, surprised that Sly hasn't started dinner. I walk to the fridge, where I find a note secured by a Montana shaped magnet. Sly's slanted handwriting reads, 'Called into work for a short meeting. Home by noon.'

Glancing at the clock, I see that it's already 6:00 p.m. Where is Sly?

I grab my phone to call our next-door neighbor, Mrs. Mendelsohn. Maggie is probably there, and she'll be eager to come home.

Soon, Maggie bounds in and gives me a hug. "Thanks for rescuing me. Mrs. M wanted me to try her new strudel recipe. You called just in time."

"Strudel doesn't sound too bad. Even Mrs. M. can't mess that up too much." Mrs. Mendelsohn uses us as her guinea pigs to test her latest contest recipes.

Maggie wrinkles her nose. "Spinach strudel?"

I shudder.

"You should have smelled it," she says. "Yuck."

"Mm," I tease, as I set the table with three flowered plates.

"I'm tired from working today, and I don't want to cook tonight. We could offer to test it."

I laugh at the appalled expression on Maggie's face.

"Just kidding, Magpie." I ruffle her dark hair. "We're eating spaghetti tonight. Could you chop the salad for me?"

Maggie races to the sink, obviously relieved she's escaped the strudel.

We work together and soon have dinner on the table. Maggie sets out the salad dressing as Sly's car pulls into the drive.

"Perfect timing," Maggie grins.

We're happy to have such an appealing meal waiting for our sister. Sly works hard at Sinclair Construction, and I want to relieve some of the pressure. Our expectant grins fade, though, when Sly enters the kitchen. Her puffy eyes make it clear she's been crying.

"Sly, what's wrong?" I reach her first, followed by Maggie. "Did you have an accident? Are you okay?"

Sly works to compose herself.

"No, I'm fine. At least physically. I've been driving for hours, not sure what to do."

Sly's voice breaks as Maggie and I hold her.

"I'm sorry, girls, but I was fired!"

Saturday, September 1
6:30 p.m.

THE SPAGHETTI IS a congealed mess in Mamma's big yellow pasta bowl. I move it and the now slimy salad to the counter and rejoin my sisters at the table. It's hard to believe just thirty minutes ago I'd been anticipating a delicious dinner. Now the lingering aroma is nauseating.

Maggie is a little ball of misery on Sly's lap. Her sniffles are the background music for the scene that replays in my mind. Sly had shocked us with those three simple words: I was fired. But the words that came next were devastating.

"Robert Sinclair accused me of stealing money from the company." Sly's voice had trembled with rage. "He said if I make arrangements to repay the money, he might not press charges. Otherwise, I could go to jail."

Sly and I had been so intent on our conversation we'd forgotten Maggie was in the room. But her deep sob at the word, 'jail', had us moving to gather our little sister in our arms. Eventually, Sly had lifted Maggie's slight weight and sat down to hold her while the emotional storm raged.

"Will Jess and I have to live with strangers?" Maggie's whispered words draw me out of the memory.

Sly and I exchange startled looks over Maggie's head.

"No, of course not." Sly's words are infused with assurance, but Maggie pushes away.

I watch as Sly gently guides Maggie upstairs, whispering words of comfort.

"But how can you know for sure?" Maggie's words echo down the stairway and my heart breaks at the bleakness in her tone. She's only eleven years old and already she's lost too much.

My fault. I shake my head, trying to dislodge the accusation of my mind. My heart. I can't think about that right now. I force myself to concentrate on today's crisis, and as terrifying as it is, I almost welcome the distraction. I can't change the past, but maybe I can do something to stop the devastation of our future.

2

Saturday, September 1
11:45 p.m.

Wind whips my face as I race across the pasture on Chieftain. As if Cole would ever let me ride the stallion, but hey, this is a dream. In the next minute, I'm trying to identify the noise that woke me. Lying still for a moment, I pray it's just a cat outside or maybe a thunderstorm. There it is again. I throw back the covers and fly down the hall, where I plow into Sly.

Her short, spiky hair pokes out in all directions, and at any other moment, I might tease her. She seems exhausted, and I hate to think of her losing another night's sleep.

"I'll go." I can barely hear Sly's quiet whisper above the increased sounds of our little sister's sobs.

"We'll both go." I lay my hand on Sly's arm and give it a slight squeeze.

We hurry to Maggie's room and open the door to discover her curled into a tiny ball in the middle of the bed.

"Magpie." Sly softy uses our father's pet name as Maggie launches into her arms, nearly knocking Sly to the floor.

"I want Mamma and Daddy!" Maggie wails.

I wish I could wail right along with her. Settling beside her, I stroke circles on Maggie's back as Sly soothes her with sounds more than words.

"Sweetheart, I know. We all do," Sly says.

Hot tears sting my eyes, and I flick them aside. I have to be strong. There will be time for crying later.

Within a few moments, Maggie's sobs dissolve into tiny hiccups. I snag a tissue from the bedside table, then offer it to her. The tension in the room lifts, and I sense rather than hear Sly's deep sigh. We've weathered another storm. Together.

"Sly?" Maggie's voice sounds strong, considering how hard she'd been sobbing earlier.

"Hmm?" Sly brushes back a damp strand of hair from Maggie's face.

"Why did God kill Mamma and Daddy?"

For a flash, I can't breathe, and I meet Sly's startled gaze over Maggie's tousled head.

"Do you mean, why did they die?" Sly asks gently.

"No!" Maggie sits up abruptly and focuses on Sly and then me. "Why did God kill them?"

"Magpie," Sly closes her eyes.

But Maggie shakes her head. "No, don't call me that. I want to know why God killed our parents. Pastor Jeff always tells us how much God loves us, but I don't believe that anymore. He can't love us if He did such a bad thing."

I study Sly, guilty that Maggie is the one to voice the question that's been tormenting me. I desperately hope Sly offers an answer—for both of us. But it's a lot to ask of a young woman who is barely twenty-two-years-old.

"Maggie, I can't answer all your questions, and we may never learn the answers until we get to heaven someday. Sometimes bad things happen, even to Christians. But I can tell you, God does love us. He wants you to tell Him how you feel—it won't make Him angry or hurt His feelings."

I'm surprised by the wisdom in Sly's words.

"Psalm 147:3 has become my favorite Bible verse in this past year. It says, 'He heals the brokenhearted and binds up their wounds' (NIV). You, and I, and Jess—we're brokenhearted. We continue with our lives, but in our own way, we're still broken. But God cares for us so much, He put that scripture in the Bible, so we'll have hope that He is healing us. Mamma and Daddy raised us to trust that God keeps His promises. He will keep this one, too."

Maggie is silent for a minute, then reaches up to touch Sly's cheek, which is wet with tears. "Okay," Maggie whispers. "I'll talk to Him about it. And I'll try to believe."

Moments later, I follow Sly out of Maggie's room, and without speaking, we both head down the stairs. The Hello Kitty nightlight glows in the kitchen and allows Sly just enough light to see as she pulls out a tin of chamomile tea. She glances at me, and I nod.

She fills two mugs with water and places them in the microwave. I move to the pantry and return with a package of peanut butter cookies, which earns a nod from Sly. She's shivering a little, so I grab a lightweight sweater and hand it to her. As Sly cocoons herself in the gray knit, I'm struck by how thin she's become.

At five foot seven, Sly has always been 'willowy,' as Mamma called her. But Sly has lost many of her curves in recent months. I wish I could share some of mine with her. I'm barely five-three, and, in my opinion, I have plenty of curves to spare.

When our snack is ready, we sit and sip our drinks, neither willing to break the silence. The kitchen is my favorite area in our home. The cheerful yellow curtains and Mamma's brightly colored woven rugs make it welcoming and cozy.

In the evenings, Daddy often worked at the kitchen table, keeping Mamma company as she graded papers for her third-grade class. Over the past months, Sly has taken their place at the table, working into the night to pay bills and manage our small household.

Ten months ago, we sat at this kitchen table, absorbing the news that our parents were dead. How was it possible? They'd been laughing when they climbed into Daddy's car that afternoon. A few hours later, they died when their car skidded on standing water and plummeted into a ravine.

"Do you ever get mad at God because of what happened?" I blurt. "I mean, I know we get angry that Mamma and Daddy died. But it affected your entire life. You quit college and changed your plans so you could become our guardian. It isn't fair to you." My voice trails off as I speak the words I've been holding in for ten long months.

Sly sips her tea. "It isn't fair to any of us."

"But you were only twenty-one years old," I say. "You should be in Missoula, at college, studying photojournalism and engaged to Brad Jenkins. Instead, you moved home to take a job at Sinclair Construction. You gave up your dreams." I contemplate my cooling tea and wonder if reminding Sly of everything she's lost is the right way to repay my sister for her sacrifice.

"Who says I gave up my dreams? I will be a photojournalist, but it may take a little longer to earn my degree. I'm learning interesting techniques through the online courses I'm taking. And I liked my job most of the time." She flashes a sad smile.

"Trust me, Brad is no great loss. He started hanging out with some real partiers, and it affected our relationship. I was already considering breaking off my engagement with him. Please don't worry about me, Jess." Sly puts her hand on mine. "God's got a plan for each of us. It will be okay. And I'll find another job."

I wish I can feel as confident as Sly. Our parent's death has shaken my faith more than I prefer to admit. And while I don't believe God killed them, I can't seem to find a solid footing with my faith these days.

It reminds me of the song I used to sing in Sunday School about the man who built his house on the sand. When the storm came, his house fell down. These days, I have an uneasy feeling that the ground beneath my faith is as shaky. I just hope there are no more storms.

Sunday, September 2
8:00 a.m.

I OPEN MY EYES, and for a moment, everything seems the same. My Tweety alarm clock reads eight o'clock, and the sun is peeking in my bedroom window. But gradually, the events of last night force their way into my consciousness.

What if I can't prove Sly's innocence, and she goes to jail? Our only relatives are Grandma and Grandpa Thomas, and they live in a nursing home in Florida. Sly tried to reassure us last night, but the reality is, Maggie and I might have to go into foster care. We could even be placed in different homes. My heart pounds as I consider that possibility.

I brush aside the negative thoughts as they race through my mind. Sly is innocent. That's all there is to it.

Before we returned to our beds last night, Sly and I agreed to keep today as normal as possible for Maggie's sake.

Sliding out of bed, I pull on a black skirt with a baby pink T-shirt that shows off my fading summer tan. I gather up my long hair in a loose ponytail and hurry down the stairs, pulling on my pink Vans as I go.

Sly is sitting at the kitchen table, still wearing the black yoga pants and old sweatshirt she changed into last night. Did she even go to bed?

She glances up as I enter the room. "There's fresh coffee if you want some."

I nod and pour myself a cup. I prefer Pepsi to wake me up, but today, coffee suits my mood. I sit next to my sister and give her arm a squeeze.

"It will be okay," I reassure her. "I talked to Cole last night, and he says Nick will do everything possible to get to the bottom of this." Because Justice is such a small town, law enforcement consists of Sheriff Harvey Richards and Deputy Sheriff Nick McBride.

Sly gives a tiny smile. "Yes. Nick called last night when you were sleeping. He convinced Robert not to press charges yet. At least he saved me from the humiliation of being taken to the police station. He plans to stop by later this afternoon to ask me a few questions."

She blows into her coffee, then whispers, "Jess, I don't know what I'll do if I lose you and Maggie, too. I promised Mamma and Daddy I'd take care of you two girls if anything ever happened to them. I can't let them down." Tears glimmer on her lashes, and she swipes them aside.

"You listen to me, Sylvia Rae Thomas," I say fiercely. "You haven't let anyone down, not Mamma and Daddy, and certainly not Maggie and me. You gave up so much to live here in Justice with us. When this mess gets straightened out, the Sinclairs will owe you a sincere apology. As a matter of fact, I think I'll insist they rent the billboard on Interstate 15 and post it there!"

Sly smiles at my vehemence. "You're probably right. It's a horrible misunderstanding. Besides, Nick is a good investigator. Remember last summer when the Benson brothers broke into homes while the owners were on vacation? Nick was determined to catch them in the act, and he did."

"That's right. Cole says he's never met anyone as stubborn as his brother. " Then I remember the rest of his statement. "Well," I add self-consciously, "he did say except for me."

She looks into my eyes. "Jess, I love your loyalty to me, but you'll need to keep your temper in check. Please let Nick do his job, and you stay far away from the Sinclairs until this is resolved, okay?"

I give a non-committal grunt as I pour a bowl of cereal for myself and Maggie, who can be heard thumping down the stairs.

As she enters the room, I'm relieved to see her usual infectious grin, and my tension eases a bit more.

"You're right on time," Sly says as Maggie joins us at the table. "You can say grace."

"Grace."

Maggie and I speak at the same time, and Sly tries to give us a stern look but fails.

"Pray, please," she says, twitching a smile.

"Father, thank you for this beautiful day. Please bless this calorie-free food. Amen." I pick up my spoon and focus on my Sugar Smacks.

"Calorie-free?"

I shrug. "Hey, last week, Pastor Jeff read that scripture, 'You have not because you ask not.' I thought it was worth a try."

Sly opens her mouth to say something, then appears to reconsider. She shrugs and spoons up some oatmeal.

"Hey, Jess, could you curl my hair this morning for church?" Maggie asks around a mouthful of cereal.

Sly and I both stop eating, with our spoons half-way to our mouths.

Reaching over, Sly touches Maggie's forehead. "No fever."

I look into Maggie's dark brown eyes. "For real, Magpie?"

She nods with enthusiasm, and her long russet braid swings forward toward her bowl. I rescue it in the nick of time. I definitely don't want to curl sticky hair.

"What's the occasion?" Sly says.

Maggie stares at Sly as if she is from outer space.

"This is the day," Maggie says. At our puzzled stares, she sighs and mutters something that sounds like *clueless*.

"The day?" I tease.

Maggie gives me a patient look and speaks as if she's talking to a toddler. "Today, I will join the junior high Sunday School class."

The light dawns, and I give Sly a guilty glance. We forgot Maggie's special day. Today, our Sunday School is starting a new series for the year. Maggie will turn twelve at the end of the month, but the leaders have invited her to be part of the class from the beginning so she won't miss any lessons. Maggie has looked forward to this day all summer, but we were so overwhelmed with Sly's news, we completely forgot.

"I'll be happy to curl your hair, Magpie," I say, honestly.

She grins and returns to her cereal. Maggie is small and compact, which helps her excel in her gymnastics class. Her long brown hair has natural highlights of red and gold, and she has a scattering of freckles across her nose. She's adorable.

Sly's gaze mirrors the same love and concern for our little sister. Tears sting my eyes. We're Maggie's only family now. It isn't right. Mamma and Daddy should be here, at this very minute, sharing our breakfast. They should be hugging Maggie and telling her how proud they are of her. Now that responsibility—and honor—belong to Sly and me.

"Please, God," I whisper in my heart. "Please help us."

Sunday, September 2
12:00 p.m.

AFTER CHURCH, I meet up with Grace and Cole. Grace spent the morning working in the nursery, and she looks like she needs a nice, long nap.

"What's cooking?" I ask my typical after-church question and receive the typical responses.

"Taco Bell," says Cole.

"Wendy's salad," says Grace.

"McDonald's." Maggie appears next to me, jumping up and down in excitement.

"Um, Magpie," I say, considering a diplomatic way to un-invite my little sister to lunch.

"The junior high class is driving to McDonald's in Dillon, and Sly says we're going, too." Maggie dances away on happy feet.

"Let's skip McDonald's," suggests Cole.

"No doubt," Grace agrees.

We decide on the Dairy Barn, at my suggestion.

"Hey, they'll close next month, so we need to get our fill of chili-cheese fries while we can."

We scrunch into Cole's truck and head to the edge of town.

Grace keeps glancing at me, silently asking if I want to discuss Sly, but I shake my head, my throat tight. Cole's mouth looks grim, but he stays silent.

Last night, I'd called first Grace, then Cole to explain Sly's problem. Shocked and angry, they promised to pray for the truth to come out. I appreciate their support, but I need to forget— even for a few minutes.

When we arrive, we discover that others from our high school BoB—Bunch of Believers—group decided to eat here, too.

Todd Sanderson stands up and waves at us. "Hey, guys, over here."

We order our food and soon join Todd, his sister, Terri, and a girl I've never met before. However, I noticed her sitting with the Sanderson family at church that morning. We settle onto the vinyl benches.

"This is our cousin, Macy, from Tennessee," Todd says. "She's staying with us for a while."

Macy has tawny brown hair and blue eyes that remind me of robin's eggs. She resembles her cousins, which means she is beautiful. Not that Todd is beautiful. Well, maybe a little. Macy is unlike them in one way, though.

Todd and Terri, seventeen and fifteen, are both very outgoing. Macy seems to be the opposite of outgoing. Is there such a thing as ingoing?

We introduce ourselves to Macy, and she gives us a timid

smile but doesn't say a word. In fact, we're half-way through lunch before Macy proves she can actually speak.

"Could you show me the bathroom?" she whispers to Terri.

Terri nods, and I see Todd watching them with concern.

"Everything okay?" Cole asks.

Todd appears startled we're still there. "Um, sure. I mean, of course." His grin seems genuine.

By the time we leave, the weirdness evaporates. But I have an odd sense that Macy could use a friend.

3

Sunday, September 2
2:00 p.m.

Cole drops Grace at the Ellison home so she can babysit their four-year-old twins, Janey and Joey. I agree to help her later after I work on my algebra homework, so Cole drives the truck from the Ellison's to my house. He wisely chooses not to discuss Sly's problem, probably because he can tell I might burst into tears at any minute if he does.

I hop out practically before he stops the truck, and as I close the door, I catch a glance at his puzzled look. He must be wondering why I'm avoiding the subject of Sly. I kind of wonder that myself.

Shrugging out of my church clothes, I change into soft, black leggings and a huge, maroon University of Montana sweatshirt that belonged to my dad. *Grizzlies* is written across the front, and there's something comforting in wearing it.

Two minutes into my algebra homework, I start to nod off. My sleepless night is catching up with me, so I ride my bike over to the Ellison's to help Grace with the twins. There will definitely be no sleeping there.

"Gracie." I open the Ellison's front door and call out to my friend, "Are you in here?"

"Upstairs." A muffled reply drifts down from above, and I hurry to the stairway. The twins are notorious troublemakers, and I wouldn't be shocked to discover Grace tied up while Janey and Joey do a war dance around her.

Turning right at the top of the stairs, I enter the twins' room, which normally looks like it belongs in a decorating magazine. A large bunk bed is along one wall, a ladder and slide are attached to the end rail.

Mrs. Ellison is very particular about keeping the room clean and uncluttered, but I guess the twins didn't get the memo. Toys and games litter the floor, and a partially finished craft project lies scattered across the child-sized table. On the opposite wall is the latest masterpiece of Janey, the Ellison family artist.

The Ellison's have read the most recent books detailing how to encourage imagination and not stifle creativity. As I study the painting, I notice there is no paper on the wall. Janey has painted her picture directly onto the plaster. I touched the tip of my little finger to a smear of bright, yellow paint. Still wet.

Real creative, our little Janey. Apparently, painting on paper would be too stifling.

I search around for Grace with no luck. A moment later, I hear a muted version of her voice. Crossing to the closet, I thrust aside a chair, which has been jammed under the doorknob. I open the door to find Grace huddled inside, face red with anger.

"Are we having fun yet?" I grin down at my clearly furious friend.

"Where are they?" Grace stands and slides through the opening in the closet door. Not bothering to respond, she races down the hall. "I've had it with those two. We were playing hide-and-seek, and they trapped me in the closet."

In a totally different tone, she sings out sweetly, "Oh Jaaaney,

Joooey, where are you? I give up. You've outsmarted me again. Come on out, you little brats ... er ... sweethearts."

Childish giggles lead us to the master bedroom. Grace rattles the doorknob. It's locked.

"C'mon, darlings," she continues to sing-song through gritted teeth. "The game's over now. Let me in. Jess is here to play with us."

A moment later, the door swings wide, and dark blue eyes peer up at Grace and me.

"Jess?" Janey looks around cautiously. "You didn't bring Cole, did you?"

In the background, we can hear Joey whisper, "Janey, is Cole out there, too?"

"No, he didn't come this time." I push open the door to the Ellison's master bedroom and survey the damage. The king-sized bed has been turned into a trampoline; bedclothes lay in rumpled piles around the room. Through the connecting door to the master bathroom, I notice the twins must have been playing 'beauty shop' with their mother's cosmetics. I groan. A typical day at the Ellison home.

Grace stands in the doorway, opening and closing her mouth, clearly at a loss for words.

Joey peers up at her. "Janey, look! Grace looks like Goldie."

I bite back a smile. Grace does resemble their pet goldfish a little.

"C'mon, Grace, I'll help you clean up this mess." I herd the twins into their room. For once, they comprehend they've gone too far. They remain quiet on the bed as Grace and I consider a battle plan.

"Grace, why don't you clean the bathroom." I try to sound cheerful. "I'll take Janey and Joey downstairs and make them a snack. Afterward, they can watch a movie until their parents get home, and we'll tackle the rest of the mess."

My friend speechlessly turns and stalks toward the bathroom. Poor Grace. She deserves combat pay.

The Ellison's kitchen gleams white. Obviously, the twins haven't been in there yet. I sternly usher the kids to chairs and proceed to make peanut butter toast. They sit, subdued for a moment.

"Grace said you were with Cole," Janey says. "Why didn't you bring him with you?"

Several times Cole kept me company when I sat for Janey and Joey. In his words, the twins don't need a babysitter—they require a corrections officer.

"Cole's busy." I slather peanut butter on two pieces of toast and place the plates in front of the pint-sized demolition crew. "I'm sure he'll be sorry he missed the excitement, though." I grin as a look passes between them. While the twins are crazy for Cole, they also know what he would say concerning them locking Grace in the closet and making such a mess.

"That's okay," says Janey with a wave of her tiny hand. "We'll see him another time."

"Yeah," Joey repeats with a measure of relief in his voice. "Another time."

Three hours later, Grace and I sit at my kitchen table. Grace has recovered her usual sense of humor as we discuss the twin's destructive habits.

"D'ya think they lay awake at night, thinking up ways to drive me crazy?" she asks in her soft southern drawl.

"Don't worry. You've lasted longer than most of the Ellison's babysitters."

Last year, Grace's father transferred to Montana from Atlanta, Georgia, and she started attending Justice High School. Grace's accent always fascinates me. Sometimes, I attempt to talk like her, but I sound like Alvin the Chipmunk. The combination of her accent, strawberry-blonde hair, and blue eyes is attractive.

But there's also something restful in Grace. While I've often been compared to a tornado, she's a calm summer breeze that gently swept in during the worst time of my life. Sometimes, I wonder if God sent Grace to Justice, Montana, just for me. She tempers my schemes with her voice of reason. Not that I always take her advice, but it's nice to have it.

The only time I've ever witnessed her even temporarily ruffled is when she deals with the Ellison twins.

"At least the Ellison's don't blame you for the mess. They must be aware of what their own children are like. The way I look at it, if they come home to find the twins are healthy and the house still standing, you've accomplished your job."

I raise my can of Pepsi, and Grace meets it with her Mountain Dew.

"To a job well done," she declares with a grin. "Now, speaking of a job well done, how did the driving lesson go yesterday?"

I groan. "I don't want to discuss it. I almost wrecked Cole's truck three times."

"Ouch," Grace says. "What did Cole say?"

"I'm not sure," I reply with a frown. "Most of it was in Sioux." I hook my foot through the chair spindles and settle in to tell her all about my day with Cole.

Grace laughs as I conclude the story. "Uh oh, did you make that vein stand out in his neck?"

"Oh, yeah," I smirk.

"Cole is right about Mark, though."

I cringe. "I wouldn't get in a car with Mark Crowley."

"I know that. I mean, it's not smart to make Cole jealous of Mark."

"But I'm not!" I protest.

Grace raises an eyebrow.

"Well, okay," I admit with a shrug. "But Amy was there and went for a ride with Cole."

Grace's eyes narrow at the mention of Amy's name.

"I can't bear the thought of her latching on to him." I justify myself, "Besides, Cole knows I'm teasing." I nibble on my lower lip. "You think he knows that, right?"

Grace gives me a reassuring nod. "Maybe. It might be a good

idea to remember that Cole isn't the kind to play games. Have you considered it's time to tell him how you really feel?" Grace watches me, and when I don't answer, she continues, "But there's something else you should keep in mind."

"What's that?"

"If you do play games, Cole might decide to make a few rules of his own."

4

Wednesday, September 5
6:30 p.m.

I love Wednesdays because of BoB. Bunch of Believers meets at Pastor Jarrod and Anna Moore's home, a renovated farmhouse located five miles from town. They moved to Justice when he inherited the house from his grandmother two years ago. Soon after, they began attending our church, became the youth pastors, and BoB was formed.

Cole picks me up at 6:30 p.m., and we travel the two miles to Pastor Jarrod and Anna's place. We haven't talked since Sunday's lunch at the Dairy Barn.

"You look tired," Cole observes.

Excellent, just what a girl wants to hear. "I am tired. Maggie had another nightmare last night. Even after she fell asleep, Sly and I were up late making plans to help her. On the nights she doesn't wake us, I still can't relax because I'm listening for her." Tears sting my eyes, and I glance out the window before Cole can notice them.

"Maybe she should see a counselor. I mean, she was barely eleven when your parents died."

I bristle a little at the idea we haven't tried helping Maggie. Noticing my reaction, Cole holds up one hand.

"Ah, so you're already on that. What does her counselor say?"

"Our counselor," I correct. "Dr. Barnes is a family counselor we started seeing the week after the accident. Pastor Jeff recommended her, and the church even pays the fees. She's great."

Cole appears surprised. "I didn't know you're seeing a counselor."

I grin, attempting to lighten the mood. "What, you think I'm this well-adjusted all on my own?"

He smirks. "Something like that."

"Anyway, Sly called Dr. Barnes today, after Maggie's latest nightmare. We meet with her next week. I sure hope she can help. I hate to see Maggie so upset. Besides, I fell asleep in French class this afternoon and just missed landing on the floor. Thank goodness, Grace caught me while Madame Fellini's back was turned."

"You owe Grace big time. You'd be conjugating French verbs until Thanksgiving if Madame caught you sleeping."

I reach into my small bag, removing a chocolate bar as we approach the farm. "Grace's reward. I wonder if Macy will be here?"

"Maybe." Cole turns onto the dirt road heading to the Moore's farmhouse. I wait for more information, but Cole can be a clam when he chooses.

"Didn't you hang out with Todd on Sunday night? Did he tell you anything about Macy and how long she's staying?" I try for casual curiosity. I fail.

Cole gives me a look that suggests he's aware I'm digging. He appears to consider several options, then he responds in true Cole-like fashion, "Nope."

His mouth twitches. He's obviously aware his lack of information frustrates me. In fact, I'm sure he knows more regarding Macy's situation than he's telling, but Cole hates gossip. Which this is not.

"Fine." I shrug. "Be that way."

Cole grins as he parks the truck in front of Anna's lilac bush. "I will."

I roll my eyes and hop out of the truck. Laughter floats from the house; BoB is in full swing. Cole opens the screen door, and I step into Anna's roomy kitchen with its soothing pale blue paint and white cabinets.

Pride fills my heart, since I was part of the crew that helped pull up the old linoleum that revealed a beautiful hardwood floor. Sly is one of Anna's closest friends, and they spent hours visiting flea markets and antique shops, discovering the perfect accents for the house.

I love the fireplace that's accessible to the kitchen and the family room. Pastor Jarrod and Cole's brother, Nick, replaced the crumbling bricks with cobalt blue tiles, and it looks amazing.

Grace stands in the corner, chatting with Kellen Stone, a junior who's recently started attending BoB. Kellen's church doesn't have a youth group, and Grace's brother, Matt, invited him to join us. Kellen has seamlessly meshed with our group. Tonight, Kellen is wearing one of his typical funny T-shirts. This one reads, *Due to unfortunate circumstances, I am awake.*

Grace waves me over with a hand holding half a cider donut.

"Jess, Kellen is telling me about the mod he designed for Minecraft. It already has 1,000 views on YouTube."

"Um, cool," I say. I'm familiar with Minecraft and YouTube. Mods, not so much.

"Can I borrow you for a minute?" I grab Grace's arm and tug.

"Could you excuse us, Kellen? We can talk more later, though, okay?" Grace offers him her best smile.

I pull her into the laundry room and close the door.

She frowns at me.

"What?" I ask in surprise. "You didn't want to be rescued?"

"Kellen is funny and interesting, and I was enjoying talking to him."

Her nose twitches as she attempts to identify the odor in the room. I indicate the bottle of fabric softener sitting on the washing machine, and she nods, then crosses her arms and resumes her glare.

"Well, I guess I missed the signals. Anyway," I continue, dismissing Grace's pout, "I wonder if Macy is coming tonight? Have you learned any more about her?"

Grace raises one eyebrow. "I didn't realize I had an assignment. What do you want to know?"

"I'm not sure," I admit.

"There's an old-fashioned way to learn information about someone. It's called conversing. With. Them."

Grace gazes at the laundry room door, and I suppose she's mentally discussing mods with Kellen.

"I tried that at lunch Sunday. But she hardly said a word and kept glancing around for an escape route."

I've captured all of Grace's attention now.

"Jess. There's a difference between a mystery and a secret. If you're friendly to Macy, she'll relax and open up a little. But show her you're interested in her, not her mystery or secret."

The clanging of the antique dinner bell hanging outside the laundry room is so loud and unexpected, Grace and I yelp and grab each other. We hear Pastor Jarrod's voice through the laundry room door.

"OK, BoB-ites, let's get started. Grab your food and head to the family room."

"I need to find a good seat." Grace opens the laundry room door so fast that Pastor Jarrod jumps.

We stare at each other in shock.

He nods toward the laundry room, "No starch in my socks, next time, please."

Grace snickers and races off to grab her favorite seat near the fireplace. I make a quick trip to the kitchen, snatching the last cider donut.

A few minutes later, Pastor Jarrod has us all settled down and paying attention. "Hi, guys. I hope you've all had a good week so far."

A chorus of agreements and groans echoes around us, and I'm relieved when I see Macy. She's sitting scrunched down in the leather sofa between her cousins, looking like she wants to escape. But at least she's here.

After announcements, Caleb, our worship leader for the evening, strums his guitar. We sing, "What a Beautiful Name," and I relax, letting the stress leak out of me a little. I've thought about Maggie's nightmare and our conversation many times since Sunday night. Now tears sting my eyes as I remember her words, 'Why did God kill our Mamma and Daddy?'

Public crying is not my favorite activity, but this family room has become a sanctuary of sorts. I realized in the early days after our parents died that I couldn't sit here and stay stoic and unfeeling. But with the tears came the care and comfort of these friends. There were special moments when God seemingly wrapped His arms around me and held me when I sobbed out my hurt and grief. This is where my healing began.

When I open my eyes, Macy is watching me with a mixture of curiosity and compassion. I offer her a quick smile, and she ducks her head, sinking even deeper into the couch.

When the meeting ends later that evening, I wander to where Terri and Macy stand. They're staring through the large picture window at the sprawling front yard. When I approach, a barn cat is stalking something in the grass.

"Mouse?" I ask.

Macy whirls and gapes at me, her eyes huge and terrified. "What did you say?" she barely gets the words past her trembling lips.

Terri appears as mystified as I am.

I motion toward the cat, who seems ready to pounce. "Um

..." I stammer, alarmed by the look in Macy's eyes. "Maybe the cat found a mouse."

Now others in the group sense something's wrong, and Todd moves to touch Macy's arm. "Mace, are you okay?"

Tears stream down Macy's cheeks, and I worry she might become sick right there in Anna's family room. Instead, she turns and stumbles out the front door and down the wide porch steps. Through the window, I see her racing toward Todd's car.

Standing there in shock and guilt, I turn to Terri and Todd. "I'm so sorry. I didn't mean to upset her."

Terri touches my arm. "It's not your fault, Jess. She needs time to recover. We don't know what might trigger her."

Todd clears his throat, a signal for Terri not to reveal anything more.

She gives me a brief hug. "It'll be okay. We'll take her home now."

"Please tell her I'm sorry," I say, a lump lodged in my throat.

Terri nods, then she and Todd disappear through the door and jog toward the car. Soon, they're driving down the lane and back to the highway.

Cole reaches over and swipes a tear away from my cheek. "It isn't your fault, Jess."

Grace joins us. "You're right, Jess. Macy seems to have a secret *and* a mystery."

5

"Maybe you shouldn't work at Hadley's today."

Sly slathers her English muffin with a generous helping of peanut butter, and once again, I marvel that she's so slim.

"It might be a little awkward if Amy Sinclair shows up."

At the mention of Amy's name, my temper ignites, and I shoot her a glare. "The Thomas sisters shouldn't be ashamed!" I insist. "You sound like Cole. I can't believe you both want me to hide at home."

"Cole agrees with me, huh?" Sly watches me over the rim of her coffee cup.

I shrug. "He offered to give me a few days off. He said he'll tell Ben something came up. But I told him the same thing. We have nothing to be ashamed of." I stand and toss my now-cooled coffee into the sink.

"All right, if it's that important to you. But please promise me you won't argue with Amy. I know she's not your favorite person anyway, and she may use this opportunity to give you a hard time. Keep your cool, okay?"

I raise my eyebrows. "*Moi?*"

Sly shakes her head as I saunter out of the kitchen.

Thirty minutes later, the bell rings, signaling the beginning of French class. I slump into my seat, and Grace, who sits across from me, gives me a smile. A moment later, Madame Fellini sweeps into the classroom, her long skirt a riot of color. But even Madame can't distract me from my thoughts. There must be a way to prove Sly's innocence.

Seeing Macy's distress last night forced me to understand one thing. It's not healthy to keep my problems inside. I have good friends who'll listen and help if they can. Instead of pushing them away, I'll accept their support. I especially need Cole. His government class is in Dillon today, touring the University of Montana-West. He won't be back until 3:00 p.m. This will be a long day.

By mid-morning, I revise my opinion. It will be a long, frustrating day. Somehow, word leaked out concerning Sly's firing, and I'm kept busy alternately accepting my friends' support and defending my sister. Most people in town trust that Sly would never steal, but that doesn't stop the gossip.

Amy Sinclair and Tabitha Reynolds whisper in the halls, spreading lies to the other students. I try ignoring them as clanging locker doors announce the end of the school day. Eager to escape, I stuff my geometry book into my locker just as a strong arm settles across my shoulders.

"Hi," I say, turning to face Cole as I try not to react to his light touch.

We'd been friends for years and brushed against each other many times. But now, I tingle, just like after I grabbed an electric cattle fence when I was ten. Electri-fried, as Maggie would say. I turn back to my locker to cover my confusion and try to slow my heartbeat.

"Hi, yourself." He smiles, and the dimple in his cheek makes a flash appearance.

When I climb into Cole's truck, I'm ready to sob. My earlier goal of sharing my problems disappears, and a blanket of pain settles around me.

"Tough day?" Cole asks. He pulls from the parking lot and heads south on Route 41.

I swallow the lump that appears in my throat at his gently voiced question. "Not too bad," I mumble. "I can handle it."

He watches me for a minute, then nods in satisfaction. "Good. When we're finished at Hadley's, I'll ask Nick what he's come up with today. My parents plan to see Sly and offer any support they can. This will work out, Jess. We have to trust God."

I nod, and Cole's words echo in my mind, '*We have to trust God.*' But I'm not sure I can trust God anymore.

I grew up attending Sunday School and church, and God seemed like a loving Grandpa. When Mamma and Daddy died, church friends surrounded me. They held me when I cried and encouraged me to tell God how I felt. But as the days passed, I pulled away from God, asking that same painful question. Why?

Losing my parents has shaken my faith to the core, but eventually, I've healed on a deeper level, and I've started trusting God again. Now it feels like He's letting me down—again. I shake my head, working to dislodge the depressing thoughts. We can't lose Sly, too.

Cole parks the truck in the drive, and I hurry to change my clothes. Maybe if I do some physical labor, I can work off the tension that's been building.

An hour later, I survey the stable. Clean enough to eat off the floor, I think with satisfaction. At least if you're a horse. As I return the broom, I hear voices by the paddock. Amy and Tabitha stand with their backs to the stable, talking and laughing.

I turn away but overhear the words 'Thomas' and 'thief.' I

stop and turn back toward the two girls. The frustration and anger that have tormented me all day boil to the surface.

"Excuse me. What did you say?" I speak through gritted teeth.

Amy swings around to face me. From her smirk, it's apparent she knew I was nearby when she made her accusation.

"Why, I was telling Tabby your sister stole money from my family's business. I guess that's why she's called Sly, hmm?"

In two seconds, I've crossed the space to Amy. "That's a lie, and you know it!" I shake her—hard. "My sister never stole anything in her life."

"Take your dirty hands off me," Amy grits her teeth as she shoves me. "My uncle says they've been watching your sister for months, waiting to catch her in the act. She's a thief, and they'll put her in jail, where thieves belong."

As Amy turns her back, I tackle her from behind. I'm smaller but fierce, and within seconds, I have her long blonde hair wrapped around my fists. By this time, her screams have drawn spectators, and a few seconds later, I feel two strong arms lift me off Amy.

"Jess!" Cole's tone is furious. "Let her go."

But I'm beyond caring what anybody thinks, even Cole. "No! You didn't hear what she said about Sly."

He untangles my hands from Amy's hair and concentrates on keeping me from attacking her again. Tabitha kneels on the ground, comforting Amy, who lays in the dirt, crying.

"Get her out of here," Amy screams, glaring up at Cole. "I swear I'll have her arrested, too, if she doesn't leave right now."

Cole wraps one arm around my middle and carries me toward the pickup. I've been deprived of Amy, so I focus my fury on him. He grunts as the heels of my booted feet connect with his shins. Opening the truck door with one hand, he deposits me on the seat with a decided thump. I reach for the door handle.

"Don't," he growls.

I cross my arms, settling back against the cushion. Cole strides around and climbs into the driver's seat.

"Seatbelt," he snaps. The tires toss gravel and dust behind us. I sullenly fasten my seatbelt, then take a swift glance in the rearview mirror, watching Tabitha and Ben help Amy to her feet.

I peek at Cole's profile. I've never seen him so grim. It occurs to me that he might get fired because of my actions. After all, he recommended me for the job.

Biting my lip, I'm swamped with embarrassment and guilt. I've battled my quick temper all my life, but I've never assaulted anyone. Glancing down, I see a few strands of Amy's blonde hair still captured in my fingers, and hot tears form in my eyes. I rapidly blink them away, refusing to cry. That would be the ultimate humiliation.

Cole startles me when he swings off the highway and onto a gravel road. A wooden sign shaped like an arrow says *Flemings Lake*. He still hasn't spoken a word as he parks near the edge of the bluff overlooking the water. Finally, I can't stand the tension anymore.

"Are you planning to dump my body in the lake?" I offer him a weak smile at my own joke, but I'm not reassured when he doesn't respond with an answering grin. For a second, I worry he's giving the matter serious consideration.

He leans his head back against the headrest. "No." He sighs. "If anyone deserves to land in the lake, it's me. I should never have taken you out to Hadley's this afternoon. You've had a rough week, and you might say Amy isn't always very, um, sensitive."

I lift an eyebrow. "You might say." Sarcasm coats my words.

He slants me a frown. "That doesn't excuse you from what you did, though. Attacking Amy wasn't smart. First, it's not very Christian, and second, you didn't help Sly's case with the Sinclairs."

I start to protest that I don't feel very Christian today, but his last comment catches my attention. He's right. I've hurt Sly's chances for a quick resolution.

"You're right. I let my temper get away from me. Again. I didn't solve anything, and I probably made it worse." I notice my boot marks on Cole's jeans. "Um, I'm sorry for kicking you. I guess I wasn't aware of what I was doing." I feel my face flush with the lie, and I glance away, unable to meet Cole's eyes.

"Uh, huh." Cole doesn't appear convinced. "Be glad the horse trough was empty, or we might be having this conversation with you dripping wet." But his slow smile takes the sting out of the words. "C'mon slugger, let's take you home. Sly has enough on her mind without wondering why you're late.

When we arrive, Nick's squad car and Mr. McBride's car sit in the driveway. Cole settles his arm over my shoulders, and we step through the front door. Mr. and Mrs. McBride perch on the couch beside Maggie. Sly and Nick face each other like two old-time gunslingers, ready for a showdown.

"What's going on?" I ask.

Sly looks at me, then steps toward Nick, holding her hands out. "You're right on time," she announces. "Nick is arresting me."

6

"Jessica?" Mary McBride gently touches my shoulder. I'm sitting on the porch swing, staring at the mountains. I turn toward Cole's mother. She's a stunning woman, with dark eyes and glossy black hair, highlighting her Native American heritage.

"Yes?"

Mrs. McBride offered to stay with me while Cole and Maggie pick up dinner. Nick assured Sly she would return home soon, but I'm worried this is a preview. Sly in jail, Maggie and I left alone.

I scoot over, and Mrs. McBride joins me on the swing. For a few moments, we sit, listening to the cicadas drone, then she brushes my hair from my face.

"I can't imagine how you must be feeling, Jessica," Mrs. McBride says in her gentle voice. "But Nicholas will do everything he can to deliver Sly home."

I nod. At first, I was furious with Nick, but Sly explained Robert Sinclair had pressed charges, and Nick didn't have any choice but to arrest her. Robert showed the Sheriff accounts proving Sly had stolen from Sinclair Construction. Although she denied the accusation, the paperwork supported Robert's allegations. Nick had no choice but to perform his job.

Mr. McBride is posting bail for Sly, and his kindness overwhelms me. It's a relief that she'll be home tonight, but the thought of the future terrifies me.

"Jessica," Mrs. McBride interrupts my thoughts. "There's someone else you need to trust, too."

Feeling my cheeks heat, I face her and snap, "I should trust God, right? How can I do that when He made this happen to us? First, I lost my parents, and I didn't understand, but I actually sensed God's help when Judge Simmons let Sly keep us together. But now, He's taking her away, too."

Mary McBride doesn't seem offended at my outburst. Instead, she reaches out to take my hand. "Jessica, God didn't cause those things to happen. There is evil in this world that sometimes touches our lives—even Christians. God walks with us through the problem.

"Remember the story of Joseph? After his brothers sold him into slavery, he said, 'My brothers meant it for evil, but God turned it for my good.' I believe God can take this situation, as bad as it looks, and bring good."

Studying her through a haze of tears, I whisper, "I want to believe that, but I'm so scared."

She hugs me close. "I understand, sweetheart. You can tell Him that, too."

Cole's pickup turns into the driveway, and soon Maggie bounds up the front steps.

"Hey, Jess, guess what? Cole told me when I'm old enough, he'll teach me how to drive, like he's teaching you."

Mrs. McBride and I laugh at Cole's expression.

"Wait a minute, Maggie. I said if I've recovered enough by then, I'll consider it. In four years, I *might* be ready to teach the next Thomas sister."

I stand and open the screen door as Cole and Maggie carry the food into the kitchen. They unpack the containers, and the smell of Captain Cluck's Chicken wafts through the air.

"Should we wait?" Maggie asks, eyeing the mashed potatoes. It's quiet as everyone remembers why we're all together tonight.

"Let's go ahead," Mrs. McBride says, patting Maggie's shoulder. "Chicken is a great choice since it's delicious, cold or hot. And we'll warm everything else in the microwave when they get here."

Maggie places two drumsticks on a plate, covering them with foil. "Those are for Sly." Her tone is solemn. "Drumsticks are her favorite."

I give her a quick squeeze. "Smart thinking, Magpie. I bet she'll be hungry when she gets home, hmm?" I leave *if she comes home* unspoken.

We're half-way through our meal when the phone rings. I wipe my hands and grab the receiver.

"Thomas residence." Caution fills my tone as I listen for a moment and then relax. "Thank you, Pastor Jeff," I respond. "Your support and prayers mean a lot. We'll let you know what happens." I hang up the phone and smile at Mrs. McBride. "Pastor Jeff must have read the same Bible story you did. He mentioned Joseph, too."

Mrs. McBride nods as she gathers the supper dishes. "It sounds as if God wants you to believe that truth, Jessica."

"They're back!" Maggie's excited voice interrupts us.

As we walk to the living room, butterflies flutter in my stomach. Is Sly with them?

Maggie's delighted squeal answers my question. "Sly, I saved you some chicken legs."

I offer a small prayer of thanksgiving and hug Sly. When we're all seated around the table, Nick explains the next step.

"Judge Davies released Sly on her own recognizance." He spoons up a generous helping of mashed potatoes.

"What's recgo, recgog ...?" Maggie looks puzzled as she tries to pronounce the unfamiliar word.

"Recognizance," Malcolm McBride says, grabbing the potato bowl from his oldest son. "It means, Maggie, that Judge Davies trusts Sly to appear in court when they present her case."

Maggie thumps down her milk glass, and a little splashes over the edge. "Well, of course, she'll be there. Where else would she be?"

"Sometimes, people run away rather than go to court," Nick explains. "The judge trusts Sly won't do that, so he agreed she could come home."

I see a look pass between Nick and Sly, and he continues, "In the meantime, I'll do some detective work."

"Do you have an idea, Nick?" I ask, eager to discuss a plan. "The Sinclairs are lying for some reason. Maybe Amy knows what's happening. She's at Hadley's all the time, bragging about her family's big business deals. When I'm working, I might overhear her say something that could help you with the investigation."

They meet my offer with silence for two seconds.

"No way," Cole says.

"Absolutely not," Sly adds.

"I don't think that would be wise, dear." Mrs. McBride pats my arm.

"It's best to allow the Sheriff's office to handle these matters, Jess," Mr. McBride gives me a reassuring nod.

"Cool!" Maggie is oblivious to the adult's reactions.

I regard Nick, hopefully. He's wearing the same expression Cole often gets when confronted by one of my schemes.

"No." He isn't as vocal as his younger brother, though.

My expression hardens, and I'm sure my sisters recognize it instantly. Stubborn. "Please listen for a minute, Nick. I can be a big help."

"No." He munches a chicken thigh, apparently unconcerned that I'm close to exploding.

"Um, Jess, you're forgetting something," Cole speaks up. "I gave you the next few days off work, remember?" He raises his eyebrows, sending a message.

A picture of Amy flashes in my mind. She's sprawled in the dirt, screaming, 'Get her out of here!'

My cheeks flush, and I'm grateful Cole didn't regale his family and mine with the details of my fight.

"Um, yes, I guess I do remember," I mumble.

Everyone but Sly accepts my agreement. I catch her curious gaze, and I'm relieved when Nick changes the subject.

"I also don't want you to discuss your suspicions, Jess. Got it?" Nick takes a swig of tea. "If they're true, we don't want to tip off anyone."

At least Nick didn't laugh at my idea. He's been a deputy for three years, and it's widely expected he'll become Sheriff when Harvey Richards retires.

I nod my agreement and stand to help my sisters clear the table from the second meal. When we're finished, I slip out, leaving Sly and Mary McBride deep in conversation. I search for Cole and find him sitting on the porch swing. He smiles and makes room for me to join him.

"Thanks for not mentioning what happened today." I settle into the swing's smooth glide.

"That's okay," he replies. "Like I said, I should never have taken you out there today. And it's not as if you'll ever attack Amy again. Right?" he asks pointedly.

"Of course not," I promise.

"You heard what Nick told you about staying out of the investigation, right?" Cole looks straight into my eyes.

I glance away.

He repeats his question. "Right?"

"How would you feel if Nick was unjustly accused?" I ask. "Would you be willing to relax and let someone else try to clear him? No. You'd do everything you could to help."

"I get it, Jess, but this time you'll have to trust Nick. He's trained for this. I'm concerned your involvement could cause more problems for Sly, and possibly for you, too."

"Funny how many times people have mentioned the word trust today," I say. "When you're a kid, trust is automatic. Maggie worries about Sly, but she's in the backyard right now, chasing lightning bugs with her friend, Rachel. She trusts that somehow everything will work out. It seems the older we are, the harder it is to trust like that."

Cole considers my statement. "Maybe that's the reason God refers to us as little children. I think He wants that kind of trust from us."

Leaning my head against the porch swing, I feel a little tension ease away. "I'm trying."

After the McBride family leaves, Sly is mostly her usual self as she scoots Maggie upstairs for her bath. "You've still got school tomorrow, Magpie, and you need a good night's sleep."

Maggie grumbles her way up the stairs, but soon she's singing her favorite VeggieTales song, "I want my duck," at the top of her lungs. Maggie might be close to twelve, but VeggieTales are timeless.

"So, what was going on between you and Cole tonight?" Sly sits on the edge of the sofa and gives me a questioning stare. "When he said he'd given you time off from work, you looked guilty. What happened at Hadley's today?"

Reluctantly, I tell her about the fight and Amy's threat to have me arrested.

Sly's eyes widen. "Jess, I love the fact that you're such a loyal sister, but we talked this over before you left for school this morning. You promised you wouldn't let Amy get to you."

"I couldn't stand her saying those things about you, Sly. I lost my temper." My voice breaks, the events of the day crashing down on me.

She stands to envelop me in a warm hug. "It was a hard day for all of us," she agrees. "But Cole is right. Maybe you should quit working until we resolve this problem—provided you even have a job at Hadley's anymore."

I sniff. "Well, Ben does the hiring, and his word is law. He says he's pleased with my work, so I hope he'll give me another chance."

"We'll see," she says. "But for now, stay away, and do what Nick told you. Don't mention your suspicions to anyone."

"Do you think Nick can solve this, Sly?"

She blushes. "I believe if anyone can figure it out, Nick McBride can." She gathers Maggie's books from the floor. "I'm going to say prayers with Maggie, so will you lock up before bed?"

I nod as she climbs the steps, wondering what's with the blush? A moment later, I hear a faint tap at the front door. I open it. Grace stands on the porch.

"Hi," she whispers. "I waited until Cole's family left, so I wouldn't interrupt anything."

I step onto the front porch and pull her to the swing. She squeaks.

"I'm glad you're here." I lower my voice. "I need your help."

"You've got it. What can I do?"

I describe my conversation with Nick concerning the Sinclairs.

"D'ya mean he thinks the Sinclairs stole their own money?" She appears confused. "How will he prove that?"

"That's the problem. Nick needs actual evidence." I lean closer to Grace. "And I've got a plan."

7

Saturday, September 8
11:00 a.m.

"I sure hope you know what you're doing," Grace says.

My friend has voiced that same concern at least ten times since we left her house this morning.

"The plan is simple. We'll return to the scene of the crime," I explain. "Someone at Sinclair Construction is framing Sly, so we start there."

Since Robert fired Sly for alleged theft, she wasn't allowed to empty her desk. This morning I volunteered to retrieve her personal items. I felt a twinge of guilt when Sly expressed her appreciation for my thoughtfulness. But I subdued it by reminding myself that I'm doing this for her benefit.

Grace and I accepted Mrs. Compton's offer to drive us into town. Grace's little brother, Josh, needs a haircut, so we agreed to meet later at the Dairy Barn. That's the only way Mrs. Compton can coax Josh into the barber's chair.

Now, as we stand outside the Sinclair Construction offices, I question my plan.

I glance at Grace, who's dressed for the occasion in black

jeans, a black T-shirt, and black boots. She's also wearing dark sunglasses. Subtle.

"Don't act so guilty," I whisper. "Mrs. Stovall is the office manager, and she said it's fine to get Sly's things. We aren't doing anything wrong."

"Not yet," Grace mutters.

Since it's Saturday, the office building is practically empty.

"Mrs. Stovall is waiting for you." A security guard, whose name tag reads *Terrance*, points to the elevator. "Second Floor."

I've only visited Sly at work one time, and I'm glad Terrance can direct us.

The elevator dings, causing my heart to flutter. "We're not doing anything wrong," I remind myself. "There's no harm in looking for clues."

Mrs. Stovall greets us as we approach the office cubicles.

"Jess, I can't imagine what our poor Sly is going through. I'd call her, but Mr. Sinclair told the staff we couldn't contact her while the police are conducting their investigation." She shakes her head in disgust, and it's obvious what she thinks of that order. "Our sweet Sly wouldn't do such a thing."

Hope glimmers for the first time since Sly's arrest. Such unwavering faith is a balm to my hurt and fear. Maybe this is a huge misunderstanding, and soon she'll have her job back with their apologies. I'm daydreaming of a vacation with my sisters, courtesy of Sinclair Construction when Grace's small pinch interrupts me.

"I found Sly's desk." She leads me to a small cubicle.

I falter, seeing the picture holding a prominent place on the corkboard wall above Sly's desk. The photo was taken at our church two years earlier. It was Christmastime, and several families had taken advantage of the sanctuary's festive decorations for an impromptu family picture.

For a moment, I'm standing with my family, waiting our turn. Mamma brushing back my hair from my eyes. Now I can practically feel her hand on my forehead and hear her whisper, 'I love you, Jess.'

Tears sting my eyes, and I impatiently swipe them away. There's no time for sentiment now.

"Give me a holler if you need anything else, okay?" Mrs. Stovall studies me with concern then walks into the breakroom.

Grace carefully places items into the tote bag we brought. Besides the family picture, there are several drawings from Maggie and a photo of Cole and me having a snowball fight. I grin at that memory. I annihilated him.

I sit at Sly's desk, opening the drawer to reveal a bottle of aspirin, a few coins, and a chocolate bar. I add those to the bag and pull open the last drawer. Empty.

"Hey, Grace, do you see Sly's camera anywhere? She specifically asked us to bring it home."

Grace glances at the desk and surrounding area. "Nope, I don't see it anywhere. Are you sure it's supposed to be in her desk?"

"Yes, Sly said she kept it in the right-hand drawer, but that one is empty." I kneel and peer under the desk to find a lone dust ball. "Keep a lookout, will ya?" I step away from Sly's desk. There are five cubicles in the large room, and I search each one.

"What are you doing?" Grace scolds. "You said we would grab her things and leave." Panic laces her voice.

"We have to find the camera." A door with a nameplate, *Mr. Robert Sinclair,* catches my attention, and I reach for the doorknob.

"Don't you dare!" Grace stands right behind me.

I jump and scowl at her.

"Grace, this may be the last chance I have to help Sly. Someone is framing her. I need to discover who and why. Please, keep watch, okay?"

I turn the doorknob, and my heart drops. Locked, of course. I frantically try to remember the television program I watched recently where a thief uses a pin to open a locked door. I reach up to my hair and extract a bobby pin. Who knew long hair would be so handy. I bend the pin and insert it into the lock.

"Psst," Grace hisses. "Mrs. Stovall is coming."

I stick the pin in my pocket and hurry to the water fountain, where I gulp a drink. And choke.

"Are you girls finding everything?" Mrs. Stovall eyes me in concern. "I need to lock up and head home soon. Can I help you carry these things out?" She points to the bag sitting on Sly's desk.

"We've got everything now, Mrs. Stovall." I step next to Grace. "Thanks so much for letting us come on a Saturday." I heft the bag. "This isn't heavy. We'll be fine."

"Well, if you're positive." She follows us to the elevator. "You tell your sister I'm praying for her, okay? We have to trust God."

I smile again and push the elevator button.

The door closes, and Grace turns to me. "Why didn't you ask her about the camera? She might know where it is."

"Maybe," I consider. "But what if she took it? We don't want to alert her that we think there's anything wrong."

Grace snorts. "You think sweet Mrs. Stovall stole Sly's camera? Why?"

I shrug, "I don't know. But Sly insisted it's in her desk, and now it's gone. Doesn't that seem a little weird to you?"

Grace doesn't answer, but I can tell I've given her something to consider. We exit the elevator and walk to the front door.

Terrance waves us on. "Give Sly my best."

As we walk the few blocks to town, I consider the missing camera. I hate to tell Sly we couldn't find it. She'll be heartbroken.

The town square features a small park with benches offering a perfect view of the mountains. Behind the benches stands a sign that says, *Justice, Montana, established 1882*. I grimace. Justice, hah! Where is the justice for my family?

"I love this town," Grace says as we step onto the wooden walkway running along Main Street.

I admit, whenever I walk down this street, I feel transported back into a different time. Hitching posts still stand outside several buildings, a reminder of another era. Today, however, my concern for Sly overshadows the charm of our town.

"I hate to think after everything else she's lost, Sly will lose her camera, too. It was a Christmas gift from Mamma and Daddy the year before they died. Plus, she's been taking pictures for her community college class. She always takes the camera to work so she can take pictures during her lunch hour." I readjust the tote bag on my shoulder.

"Well," Grace replies as we open the door to the Dairy Barn, "I guess we have two mysteries to solve."

"Maybe," I say. "Or maybe they're the same mystery."

The diner is packed, but fortunately, Grace's mom saved us a booth. I slide next to Grace's younger brother, momentarily sticking to the red vinyl bench. I reach for the laminated menu that's propped between the ketchup and mustard bottles.

"Why do you bother with the menu," Grace teases, "you always order the same thing every time we come here."

Cindy, our server, approaches. "I know what Jess is having, but what can I get for everyone else?"

They all laugh at my expression. "Am I that predictable?"

"Only when it comes to food," Grace reassures me. "In every other area, you are totally unpredictable."

A few moments later, I add sour cream to my chili cheese fries. A tall glass of sweet tea sits nearby. I'm in Dairy Barn heaven.

"Did you girls find everything you needed from Sly's desk?" Grace's mom squirts ketchup on Josh's french fries.

"No," Grace says.

"Yes," I say.

Mrs. Compton appears confused. "Um, were you girls —together?"

"Sure," Grace says. "But we couldn't find Sly's camera, which is the most important reason we went there. So, I'm not sure how you can say we got everything?" Grace mirrors her mom's confused look.

I sink my teeth into a fry. "We found something even more important than the camera. A clue."

"What do you mean?"

Mrs. Compton moves Josh's mug of root beer as his elbow drifts toward it. Another disaster averted.

I describe the class Sly is taking at the Community College. "She usually takes her lunch and camera to the new senior center they're building on Russell Street. Sly is documenting the construction by taking pictures of each day's progress."

"Robert met Sly in the lobby and accused her of stealing the money. He wouldn't let her go upstairs, so she couldn't clean out her desk. She told me where to find the camera, but it's disappeared. I think there's a connection somehow."

Mrs. Compton frowns. "Jess, you're a wonderful sister, and I hope you can find what you need to help Sly. But please, be careful."

"Of course."

My sincere response earns an eyeroll from Grace, but her mom doesn't seem to notice. I sip my sweet tea and reassure myself I will be careful. Careful not to quit until I find the truth.

8

Sunday, September 9
8:30 a.m.

I brush my hair until it shines. Although it's September, there's still enough warmth in the day to wear a dress, and I choose my favorite. It's white, patterned with small purple violets scattered everywhere. The stem's color accents the green in my eyes. Clipping back my hair on each side, I let the waves swing loose around my shoulders.

We have many supporters at church, but I expect to be under more scrutiny today. I need the extra self-confidence that comes from looking my best.

Slipping on my flats, I race down the stairs. "Okay, I'm ready. Let's go."

Waiting patiently with Maggie, Sly looks surprised. Although I enjoy church, I'm always late. But we might be on time for coffee and donuts this morning.

I'm eager to tell Cole that Grace and I searched the Sinclair Construction office. Maybe he'll have an idea where to look for the camera.

We arrive at Cornerstone Community Church and spend a few

minutes visiting with other early birds. I'm too anxious to eat, but I see Maggie score a chocolate donut. As the worship band plays, we slip into the seats we consider ours and prepare for the service.

I love the worship band at Cornerstone. They sing hymns and contemporary songs, accompanied by an electric piano, guitars, and drums. For a few minutes, I forget Sly's problem and lose myself in worship. No matter what's happening in my life, the minute I sing songs of God's love and power, I feel calmer and better able to face the next problem.

Beside me, Sly sniffles a little as Pastor Jeff preaches about Joseph being unjustly accused and imprisoned.

"God never left Joseph for one second," Pastor Jeff declares. "Even when Joseph was stuck in prison, forgotten by everyone, God remembered him and was always working. God had a plan for Joseph's life, just as he has for us."

For the past months, Sly has been the strong one. She sacrificed her education and plans to come home and care for us. I slip my hand into hers and give a gentle squeeze. Now, I'm determined to offer her my support when she needs it most.

After the service, I locate Cole, and then we search for Grace.

"Meet me after lunch at The Rock," I whisper urgently. "We need to talk."

When our parents were alive, Sunday lunch was always an event in our home, and this is one tradition we've kept. This morning, Sly filled the crockpot with our favorite meal: pot roast with potatoes and carrots, and the delicious aroma fills the kitchen. Sly says this is our connecting time, and we usually enjoy discussing the events of the past week and sharing our plans for the coming days.

But today, conversation is brief, as we're each lost in our

concerns about the future. We barely speak as we clear the dishes in record time. Soon, I slip into jeans and a soft yellow T-shirt, then I'm riding my bike toward The Rock.

Grace, Cole, and I often meet at The Rock on Sunday afternoons. The massive boulder offers an impressive view of the Pioneer Mountains and is a favorite meeting spot for the teenagers of Justice. I climb the large flat rock and take a moment to enjoy the warmth of the sun. A stream runs nearby, and for a few blissful moments, I forget everything as I drift off to sleep.

The sound of Cole's pickup wakes me, and I sit up to see my friends arriving together. Grace sits in the front seat, with Roxie riding in the truck bed. They stop, and Cole jumps out, reaching to haul Grace's bicycle from the back.

"Don't tell me the chain slipped off again." I walk to the truck and pet Roxie as Cole adjusts Grace's bike.

"Yes." Grace blows her bangs from her eyes then clambers onto the rock. "Cole took pity on me when he saw me pushing it along Route 41."

"There you go." Cole rolls the bike over to Grace. "Good as new."

She looks doubtful but leans the bike against a tree and resumes her seat.

"So, what's up?" Cole settles down beside me.

"I think we may have a clue what's happening to Sly," I announce.

At his questioning look, I continue. "Grace and I went to Sly's office yesterday to empty her desk. She asked us to get her camera, which she always keeps in her desk drawer. She's been taking pictures over her lunch break for her photojournalism class.

"But when we got there, the camera had disappeared. I asked her about it when I got home yesterday, and she said it was definitely in her desk when she left last week."

Cole's eyes narrow. "Well, I guess she could have taken a picture of something she wasn't supposed to see."

"In Justice, Montana?" Grace scoffs. "What could she see? The worst thing that happens is when Mr. Stuben takes a Polar Bear swim in Rattlesnake Creek on New Year's Day. Or maybe she finally caught Mrs. Dickerson cheating at Bingo in the VFW hall."

"That's the thing." I frown. "She wasn't taking pictures of people. Sly is documenting the building process of the new senior center apartment building."

Cole looks intrigued. "Who's in charge of the building project?"

"Sinclair Construction."

Sunday, September 9
3:00 p.m.

COLE TOSSES both bikes in the bed of the pickup, and we all squish into the front seat. Cole and I have been arguing for the past twenty minutes, and Grace probably feels like she's hanging out with the twins.

"No," Cole says.

"Yes," I argue.

"No." Cole shakes his head to emphasize his point.

"Why not?" I ask in what I think is a reasonable tone.

Grace rolls her eyes.

"Because I say so." As soon as the words leave his mouth, Cole closes his eyes, clearly aware he's made a mistake.

"You're not the boss of me," I yell.

Despite his obvious frustration, Cole grins. "What are you? Six?"

I stare straight ahead and don't reply.

"Okay, here's the deal," he says after a minute of silence. "You're right. I'm not the boss of you. But I am the boss of my truck, and right now, my truck is taking you home. I won't drive you to the construction site, so you can climb all over and possibly get caught, or worse, hurt. When we get home, we can talk to Nick and tell him what you suspect. He'll take it from there. Period."

"Fine." I continue to stare out the window, although I'm aware of the look that passes between Grace and Cole.

A few moments later, Cole pulls into my drive and hops from the truck. He unloads our bikes, and Grace thanks him as I stomp into the house. I enter the quiet living room and see Sly curled next to Maggie on the sofa.

"Shh." Sly nods her head to indicate a sleeping Maggie.

Grace joins me, and we tiptoe up the stairs to my room.

"You weren't very nice to Cole." Grace plops on my bed and shoots me an accusing stare.

"Well, Cole wasn't very nice to me," I counter.

"He's watching out for you," she says. "I think it's kinda' sweet."

I glare at her, then turn to my closet and start digging. Soon I unearth my oldest pair of jeans and a paint-splattered T-shirt. More digging produces a ratty pair of sneakers. Yellow paint covers them from when the BoB group painted Mrs. Ferguson's house last summer.

"What are you doing?" Grace asks.

"I'm going to the construction site. Run home, change, and you can go with me." I pull on the clothes, then the shoes. Yuck, the paint made the canvas all hard and crackly.

I put my long hair in a messy ponytail and face Grace, who leans against the bed's headboard, her arms crossed.

"I'm sorry, Jess, but you must have forgotten our plans for the afternoon. You promised to help me babysit Janey and Joey while Mr. and Mrs. Ellison go to a cookout. Remember?"

I plop on the bed. "Oh, Grace, I'm sorry, I forgot. I've been so worried about Sly that I've totally taken you for granted. I did promise to help, didn't I?"

She bites her lip, obviously debating whether or not to let me off the hook. I'm sure Grace knows if she insists, I'll keep my promise to help her babysit. That way, she can be sure I won't do anything dangerous.

She holds firm. "I genuinely need your help, Jess."

I start to argue, but guilt wins. Grace always supports me and seldom asks anything in return. But I believe there's a clue at that construction site. Whatever it is will be waiting tomorrow.

"Okay," I agree. "I'll go with you."

Sunday, September 9
4:00 p.m.

"HIGHER, HIGHER!" Janie and Joey sing in chorus as Grace and I push the swings. The local grade school sits next door to the Ellison home, and the twins think the equipment is their own personal playground.

We're discussing a snack break when we hear a loud motor rev. Soon, a black Z28 Camaro appears in the parking lot, driven by Mark Crowley.

"Hi. What are you two doing?" Mark climbs out of his car and waves us over. Janey and Joey slide behind Grace's back and peek out at him.

"Who's that?" mumbles Joey.

"Trouble," Grace whispers back.

I frown at her, then walk toward Mark. "Hey, Mark, I heard you got a new car— cool!"

"Yeah, for my birthday. I need something for dates, instead of that old junker."

Mark is Justice High's star football player. His long, curly brown hair often falls into his eyes, and I've occasionally thought of offering him my barrettes.

Since Mark's 'old junker' is a five-year-old Dodge Ram, I don't feel very sympathetic. Grace rolls her eyes, but I continue to fake-smile at Mark.

"Wanna' ride?" he invites.

"Absolutely." My reply is immediate.

"Jessica Ann Thomas," Grace warns, "don't you dare."

I give her a reassuring glance.

"Don't worry. We won't be long. I'll be back to help with the twin's baths, I promise."

"That's not what I mean, and you know it." Grace hobbles toward me, Janey and Joey attached to her legs like little crabs.

Mark leans against the car and regards us with a smirk.

"You promised Cole," she reproves.

"First, I didn't promise Cole anything. He demanded. Second, this may be my only opportunity to investigate the construction site. I'll be fine. I promise." For a second, I remember that old saying, 'don't make promises you can't keep,' but I push the thought away.

Squaring my shoulders, I turn to Mark. "Let's go."

Before she can protest anymore, I hop into Mark's car. "It'll be fine, Grace. See you soon."

Then we roar away.

Sunday, September 9
4:15 p.m.

By the time we reach the edge of town, I grasp that I've made a massive mistake. Mark is showing off, racing the engine, and running red lights. I slump in the seat, thinking it would be my luck if Nick's on duty today. I can imagine *that* conversation. Glancing at Mark, I wonder how I can convince him to slow down.

"Hey, I have an idea," I suggest, in my best wow-this-just-came-to-me voice. "Let's drive to the construction site for the new Sinclair Senior Center."

Mark shoots me a mystified glance, and I wish I'd said nothing as he takes his eyes off the road. We have to be doing 75 mph, and there are several scary curves coming up.

"Why would we want to do that?" Mark asks as he shifts the car into third gear, anticipating a hill that is fast approaching. Too fast approaching.

"Um, I don't know. I guess it would be cool to look around at all the—um—construction." Lame.

"No. I drove by yesterday, and they have a huge sign posted now. *No Trespassing*."

For a minute, I consider the irony of the situation. Even my limited knowledge of the traffic rules tells me Mark is breaking several laws right this minute. So, what's a little trespassing?

"Maybe I'll take you there later. Right now, we're gonna' take a little detour." He shifts gears again and makes a hard, right turn onto Route 278. I shoot him a quick glance and detect his smirk. Wonderful. This is progressing from awful to nightmarish.

We're speeding up the winding mountain road that leads to Bannack, a ghost town 15 miles northwest of Justice. During the day, Bannack offers tours and shows for the tourists, but I'm worried on a Sunday evening, it will be deserted. When Bannack is closed, it's a major draw for couples who want ... privacy. Why are we headed to Bannack? Duh.

"You know, Jess, I'm surprised to catch you without your bodyguard," Mark says. "Did Cole give you the afternoon off for good behavior?"

I don't like the nasty way he says Cole's name, but I ignore the taunt. "He's taking care of Chieftain at Hadley's farm."

By now, I've lost the opportunity to check the construction site since Mark has his own agenda. I reluctantly change my plan. Just getting back to town alive seems like a worthwhile goal.

"Mark." The twists and turns of the mountain road roil my stomach. "Take me home now. I'm not going to Bannack with you tonight. Or ever."

He glares at me and speeds up so abruptly I slam back against the seat.

"Too bad," he snaps. "This is a narrow stretch of road, and there's nowhere to turn around."

The speedometer registers 70 mph. Great. Now Mark is not only a jerk, but he's also an angry jerk. Not a good combination.

I pull my seat belt tighter and shut up. Everything I say

seems to make him mad, so maybe if I stay quiet, he'll come to his senses. Does Mark have senses? The jury is out.

We arrive at Bannack, and as I feared, it appears deserted. The park closed at 5:00 p.m., and although it's still daylight, the old ghost town gives me the creeps. Mark stops in front of the Meade Hotel, a two-story red brick building, and turns off the engine.

"C'mon," he says. "Let's explore."

I gape at him. "Um, no. Let's not." I frantically consider my options. If I get out, I don't trust him not to drive off and leave me stranded. Experience says I won't be able to receive a cell signal. I've visited Bannack several times for school field trips, and I usually enjoy the historic town. But those visits have included lots of other kids, teachers, and guides—sane people.

But Mark is acting so weird, friendly one minute and furious the next. I remember those girls in scary movies who check out the mysterious noises in the basement. Exploring Bannack with Mark would put me in the same category. Too stupid to live.

On the other hand, I dread the 20-minute ride down the mountain. I'm not sure which Mark will be driving—friendly Mark or psycho Mark?

I shift to face him, attempting to act calm. That's hard to do, especially since fear sweat trickles under my armpits. Gross.

"Why did you really drive me here, Mark?" I ask in my best Dr. Barnes, therapist voice. Soft. Controlled. Well-paid.

He scowls at me, not bothering to hide his anger. "Cole."

"Cole?" I repeat, even more confused. "Are you saying Cole asked you to bring me here?"

He barks a quick, loud laugh. "No. This is the last place he'd want you to be." He turns to study the abandoned buildings, obviously assuming I have all the information I need.

Think again, Mark. "Look, I don't know what you think Cole has done, but you guys can discuss it when we get back. Right now, I want you to *carefully* drive us home. In fact, I won't even mention this to Cole. We'll forget all about it." I don't add I'd prefer to keep it quiet for my own reasons.

"Nope." He shakes his head.

Mark displays the same stubborn expression Joey gets when Grace tells him to share a candy bar with Janey. I don't expect it will help to tell Mark he looks like a spoiled little boy. But I am *so* tempted.

"Cole should pay for what he did to me," he says. "Hurting you will hurt him."

Once more, I restrain myself, not pointing out Mark's cowardice in going after me rather than Cole. "Why do you want to hurt Cole?" I ask, instead.

"He got me kicked off the football team!" Mark explodes.

"What? How did he do that? He doesn't even play football." I'm more frustrated than scared.

"He told his brother, Nick, I was drinking last Saturday night, and I got arrested. Now, I'm off the team, and I'll lose my scholarship to the U next year. My dad says that's the last straw, and he's sending me to a military school. My life is trashed, and it's all Cole's fault."

I stare at him, open my mouth, then close it again. But all I can think to say is, "So, there really are military schools?"

He gapes, as if I'm the insane person in the car, and ignores my question. "Cole cares for you more than anyone else. Hurting you is the best way to hurt him."

"Hurting me, how?" I ask, brushing my fingers along the car door handle. Maybe getting stuck in Bannack is the better choice after all.

"Relax, I won't hurt you. But my friends will know I brought you here, and they'll believe whatever I tell them. And they'll make sure the entire school hears by tomorrow. Let's see how Cole likes that." He turns the ignition switch, and the engine rumbles.

Before I can say anything, we leave Bannack, and soon we're flying down the mountain. It's dusk now, but that doesn't seem to concern Mark. The curves whip by at a dangerous speed. Tires squeal as he makes the hairpin turns.

My mind races with what he's said, and weirdly enough, I keep coming back to his statement, 'Cole cares for you more than anyone else.' That's something I'll examine more when I get back home. *If* I get back home.

Mark approaches the sharpest turn on the route, but instead of slowing down, he increases speed.

Gripping the door handle, I close my eyes. *Please, God, not this way. We lost Mamma and Daddy on a winding mountain road. I can't do this to Sly and Maggie. Please, God, protect me.*

"Please, God!"

For a moment, I think I spoke those last words out loud. Then I realize it isn't my voice I'm hearing. It's Mark's.

And then we're flying.

I'M COLD. Actually, I wonder if I'll ever be warm again. The antiseptic smell of the room nauseates me, and the perpetual beeping of the monitor makes my head throb. Reaching up, I touch the gash above my eye and wince. I seriously need to sleep, but a nurse keeps checking to make sure that doesn't happen.

A concussion. I overheard one doctor say the word, and I remember from watching *Gray's Anatomy* reruns you shouldn't sleep if you have a concussion. Great. I can't escape. I'll have to be wide awake and endure every moment of this nightmare.

Flashes of remembered conversation alternate with flashes of pain. But there's a blank space between the time I was with Grace and the twins and when I woke up in the ambulance.

I read somewhere that it's normal to forget intense moments of trauma. If I'm lucky, I'll never recall the moment of impact. I remember overhearing an EMT tell someone we'd hit a tree.

I squint. I'm forgetting something very important. We. We

hit a tree. Who are 'we'? I groan and rub the bandage on my head.

"Shh," Sly's words sound close as she prevents me from pulling at the gauze.

"Jess, try to stay still." Her hazel eyes hold a depth of fear I haven't seen since the night our parents died.

"Wh-what happened? Am I in the hospital?" I mumble through dry lips.

"Yes. You've been in an accident," Sly says with the patience of someone who has repeated the same phrase multiple times. "You'll be okay. You have a concussion, so the doctor wants to keep you here tonight."

"Where's here?" I slur the words as exhaustion takes me.

"No! Jess, you can't go to sleep."

Sly's voice is louder now, and I frown at her. At least I try to frown. I'm too tired to move my mouth, so I decide I'll simply frown in my mind.

"You're at Barrett Hospital in Dillon. Thankfully, the doctors don't think you'll need transferred to St. James Hospital." Concern fills her hazel eyes.

I shiver, hearing the name of the hospital where my parents were taken after their accident. Sly notices and takes my hand, carefully not touching the IV attached to my arm.

"It's okay now, Jess. You'll stay overnight, so they can monitor you, but you'll go home tomorrow."

A thought tugs at my consciousness, and I try to focus. I need to ask a question, but I can't remember what it is.

A noise causes me to look around, and I see Maggie, Nick, and Grace crowded into the doorway. Grace's arms wrap around Maggie's waist, supporting my little sister as she shakes with fear and shock. I groan, heartbroken that my foolish actions have put that terrified look on Maggie's face.

"What's wrong?" Sly says in alarm. "Do you hurt anywhere else?"

I shake my head and then regret it when pain shoots through my skull.

"I'm so sorry," I whisper. Again, that wayward thought flies around my brain, as if my head shake brought it to the surface. What am I forgetting?

"Mark is on his way to St. James," Nick says.

Mark! I jerk upright and then let out a yelp as the IV tugs my arm. Ouch.

Nick steps next to Sly. "Mark broke his arm in the accident, but they sent him to Butte because they're concerned there may be internal injuries." He delivers the information in his cop's voice. "God must have His angels watching over you both, because that car—"

Sly touches his arm and gives a slight shake of her head, nodding toward Maggie.

"The good news is," Nick clears his throat, "you'll both be fine, eventually. Thank God."

I bite my lip as tears threaten. I'm sure of what Nick was going to say before Sly stopped him. It's only by the grace of God that Mark and I weren't killed.

Maggie gives a small whimper and pulls away from Grace, hurrying to my bedside. She gently lays her head on my shoulder, and I can feel her tears soaking through my ugly hospital gown.

A movement at the door captures my attention. Cole stands rigid in the doorway, his expression a mixture of fear and fury. Our eyes meet for a brief second, and then he walks away.

10

Monday, September 10
3:20 p.m.

"Anybody home?"

I open my eyes and shift in the recliner where I've spent the last several hours in the same static position. After being released from the hospital earlier today, Sly has barely left my side. Eventually, I convinced her to take a nap and make up the sleep she lost last night.

Now, Grace stands in the doorway, holding my makeup assignments. "Can I come in?"

"Sure." I bite my lip.

Grace sets the books on the table fitted between my chair and the picture window showcasing our backyard. Daddy and Mamma spent many hours cultivating the space—Daddy with vegetables, and Mamma with flowers. Our garden had been a family project, and I miss it.

"Grace."

"Jess."

We speak at the same time.

"Me, first," I say, scooching myself up a little straighter

against the backrest. "Grace, I'm so sorry. What I did was stupid, and you tried to stop me because you care about me." I instinctively reach my hands out to her. "Will you forgive me?"

Grace hurries over and drops to her knees beside my chair. "Of course. Jess, I was so worried." She hugs me gingerly. "Are you okay? I can't believe you hit a tree. I'm so glad you were wearing a seatbelt. Are you sure you're okay?" She studies me but doesn't wait before hurrying on, "I heard at school that Mark is awake now, but he's pretty banged up. He broke his arm and cracked some ribs, and he can't play football the rest of the season."

I look out the window. Mark's family must want to keep it quiet that he was already kicked off the football team.

"It's all my fault," I whisper, eyes resting on the group of weeping willows that mark our property line. I pull my gaze back to hers, remorse causing a tightness in my throat. "If I hadn't wanted Mark to drive me to the construction site, this wouldn't have happened."

Grace frowns. "Now, that isn't true. Mark Crowley is an accident looking for a place to happen. Did you tell him to drive 70 miles an hour on a mountain road?"

My eyes widen, and I squeeze the armrest, remembering that nightmarish drive. "Of course not. I begged him to slow down. But he laughed at me and called me a chicken."

"See there," she says. "And if Mark was taking you to the construction site, why were you on Route 278? That's in the opposite direction."

I study her, debating how much I should share regarding Mark's real reason for taking me up the mountain. Grace sits cross-legged near my recliner, but now she shifts to kneel beside me.

"Jess." Grace urges, laying her hand on my arm. "This is me, remember. What really happened?"

I sigh. "I asked Mark if we could go to the site, but he said no, we were making a detour first."

"A detour where?"

"To Bannack."

Her eyes widen.

"Unbelievable!" She jumps up and starts pacing. "There's only one reason guys go to that old abandoned town." She faces me, hands on her hips, eyes blazing. "That jerk!"

I wince. "Maybe we shouldn't talk bad about Mark since he's so hurt and—"

"Well, it's his own fault," Grace cuts me off in a tight voice.

I've never seen her so mad, and I have a sudden thought Mark should be thankful he isn't anywhere near Grace right now. If I do tell her the real reason Mark took me to Bannack, I'm not convinced her blood pressure can handle the truth.

We went off the highway close to Justice. There's no reason anyone has to learn where we'd been. I hope Mark was bluffing about his friends knowing his plan for revenge. I nibble on my bottom lip, a nervous habit I've had since I was little. Maybe no one will ever have to know. I try to sound casual.

"Has anyone at school asked why Mark and I were together?"

"No."

She pauses, watching me intently as if she senses I'm not telling her the whole story. Grace can be annoying like that.

"Please, let's keep it that way." I let my head fall back on the cushion, exhausted. "I feel stupid enough for even going with him." At least that much is true. I close my eyes, but I sense Grace at my side again.

"Look," she says, with quiet care, "you made a bad decision for a good reason—to help your sister. Mark's decisions and reasons were plain-old selfish."

"Well, so far, I've certainly messed up the great plan," I acknowledge, guiltily imagining Mark's injuries. "Mark's in the hospital, I'm sore everywhere, Sly is still fired, and Cole ..." My voice breaks, and I press cool fingers to my stinging eyelids, willing myself not to fall apart.

"Cole, what?" she asks.

"He won't talk to me," I whimper, rubbing the spot over my eyes, where a headache throbs. "He came to the hospital, apparently to make sure I was alive, then he left. I haven't talked to him since."

A solid knock sounds on the front door, and we both jump.

Grace stands and peeks through the curtain on the small window. "Well, it looks like you're going to see him right now."

I sit up straighter, panic racing through me. I smooth my hair back as Grace opens the door. Cole enters the room.

"Gotta' run. Tons of homework," Grace blurts, reaching down to grab her bookbag. "So, I'll scoot on home. See you tomorrow, Jess?"

At my nod, she gives me a quick grin.

She lightly punches Cole's arm and heads to the door. "Now, play nice."

Then we're alone.

My heart flutters as Cole walks toward me, his expression like stone. I can't guess what he might say, but I have a sense this conversation might be the most important we've ever had. My stomach flutters, reminding me of the time Cole and I rode the Screaming Eagle.

Cole claims the ottoman near me and sits, elbows on his knees. He clasps his forearms tightly as if stilling something unbridled inside him. For a long moment, his silence makes me squirm.

"Jess, when I found out you'd taken off with Mark, I was ..." His tone grim, he shakes his head in disbelief, "furious. I couldn't believe you would do something so reckless. When I heard the ambulance, somehow, I knew it was for you, and it terrified me. By the time I got to the hospital, I was angry and scared, and I couldn't promise which feeling would come out first, so I kept my mouth shut."

Tears sting my eyes, but I refuse to look away. There is something raw in Cole's eyes and so vulnerable in what he's saying that I can't run from his honesty.

He stands, and for a moment, I think he's going to turn and leave—again. Panic rises but then subsides as he moves next to me. He crouches down on one knee, his eyes never leaving mine as he touches my hand, so carefully it seems he thinks I might shatter. I honestly feel that fragile, like I might crumble into a zillion pieces and easily be scattered by the wind.

His fingers, light but searing, touch my hand, and I wait for him to continue.

"Jess," he says in a near whisper, "I'm not sure what God has planned for you and me, but in those few minutes, I realized something." He looks down at our hands, then up again.

I lean forward, not wanting to miss his next words.

"I never want to lose you."

Brushing at my tears, I try to swallow. "I feel the same way," I whisper. "I'm so sorry I accepted that ride with Mark. My plan was to search the construction site, but he had his own plan. I was focused on helping Sly, and I thought it was the only way to get the answers we need, and ..."

My voice trails off at his expression.

"Jess, please do something for me and my sanity," Cole pleads. "Let Nick solve the case. I think he's taking a very personal interest in it."

"You mean you've noticed, too?" The tension eases, and we're back in our comfort zone.

"Oh, yeah," he grins. "It seems like my brother and your sister are getting closer every day—and liking it. Funny how things work out. Nick and Sly have known each other since they were kids, but it took this crisis to draw them together." A thought seems to capture his attention. "Kind of like us," he says, quirking a smile. "Who knows? Something good may come out of this yet—for all of us."

A sweet memory surfaces. "Mamma always said that God is the only One who can take something the devil means for bad and turn it into something good."

Cole nods and stands. He surprises me by leaning down and

placing a soft, quick kiss on the top of my head. "Get better, Nancy Drew. I'll see you tomorrow." Then, he's gone.

I'm already missing Cole, although he just closed the door. I touch the place where he kissed me and laugh. *I may never wash my hair again.* I eventually doze, waking to the sound of raised voices coming from the kitchen.

"But you said they were considering dropping the charges." Sly's voice trembles.

"Peter Sinclair told me that's the plan. But his brother, Robert, convinced him to make an example of you." I hear the anger in Nick's voice. "Robert says they owe it to the shareholders in the company to take a hard line with company theft."

"But I didn't steal anything."

Sly is weeping now. She sounds scared, an emotion she hasn't shown to Maggie and me. The fear in her voice triggers a memory of the night when my sisters and I learned our parents died. I feel nauseated.

"Nick, someone is setting me up. Please believe me."

"Listen to me. I not only believe you, I believe *in* you. This isn't who you are. You could never do anything like this. I promise I'm doing everything I can to prove it."

"What about the construction site?" Sly asks.

My heart dances a little. Finally, someone is paying attention to my theory.

"No." Nick dismisses the idea. "We'd need a warrant to search the site, and we have no probable cause. I asked the Sinclair brothers, but Robert said no. He thinks I'm too involved, and he's asking the Sheriff to remove me from the case. That won't happen, but I need to be careful with my investigation."

My heart plummets. I stand and tiptoe to the kitchen door, watching as Nick pulls a weeping Sly into his arms. I don't need to invade their privacy any longer. I've heard enough, and I know what I have to do.

11

Wednesday, September 12
6:30 p.m.

The accident is the chief topic of conversation when Grace and I arrive for the BoB meeting on Wednesday night. Girls surround me with hugs, while the guys stand in a corner, looking grim. I overhear several of them mention Mark's name, but their words are drowned out by the girl's exclamations of concern. I note Anna giving me a look I interpret as 'Let's talk later.' Great.

Since the accident happened close to town, only Grace knows we'd driven to Bannack. I want to keep it that way. If I tell Sly, she will tell Nick, because Mark basically kidnapped me. Nick will arrest Mark, and Cole will find out Mark took me to Bannack and why. Not happening.

But watching Anna's laser focus on me, I'm afraid my secret is in danger. She's like a human lie-detector. The FBI should recruit her as an interrogator. Maybe I can fake a headache and have Grace take me home before the meeting ends and Anna pounces. I do have a head injury, although truthfully, it stopped hurting yesterday. I wince at that word: truthfully.

"Are you okay?" Grace appears in a flash. "Does your head hurt? Let's sit on the couch before the guys claim it."

Shaking my head, my bangs brush against the bandage on my forehead. "I'm fine."

We settle into the leather couch that Sly and Anna found at a second-hand store. It's as comfortable as it is ugly.

"But Anna looks like she wants to play 'Truth or Dare,' without the *dare* part. I'm worried she'll ask for details about the accident, and you know I'm a terrible liar."

Grace quirks an eyebrow. "You say that like it's a bad thing."

"Well, it kind of is." I spell out the whole Anna-tells-Sly-tells-Nick-tells-Cole scenario.

"That could be a problem," she agrees.

The screen door opens, and Todd, Terri, and Macy walk into the room, interrupting our escape plan. Their serious expressions make me wonder what's wrong. Macy was at church on Sunday morning, but she appeared to be crying through most of the worship service. She and Terri slipped out during the offering and never returned.

Tonight, Macy wears a determined expression, but she glances at me and gives a tiny smile, which I return.

They settle in front of the fireplace. It's been in the 70's today, so no fire for BoB tonight. The door opens, and Cole slips into the room, finding a seat in the corner. I have my usual reaction when Cole arrives, a mixture of happy and edgy. It's a weird sensation.

Pastor Jarrod steps into the middle of the room. "So, tonight, we'll mix things up a bit. Instead of having worship first, one of our group has something to tell us." I'm shocked when he turns to face the fireplace. "Macy, will you share your story?"

There's an expression, 'you could hear a pin drop,' and it's accurate. The only sound is the steady ticking of Grandma Moore's old clock sitting on the fireplace mantle. I can't imagine what Macy is feeling as all eyes turn to her. I would hurdle the bodies around me and run out the door.

Terri reaches over and touches Macy's hand. "This is a safe place, Macy. *We* are safe."

Macy nods and says, "My mom and I are from Tennessee." Those are the most words I've heard from her in one sentence. "Mom is a nurse, and last March, she started a new job at a hospital near Nashville. It was hard to leave the small town where I grew up, but I felt kinda' excited, too, ya' know?

"Elmore, Tennessee, is half the size of Justice, so not much happens there. I figured I'd make friends, and things might be easier for us with Mom's new job. And besides, Nashville ..." Her voice breaks, and she glances down at her lap.

"Take your time, Macy," Pastor Jarrod says.

The clock ticks off nearly twenty seconds before she clears her throat and looks around the room. "I'm a singer," she says. "I write my own songs and sing them. My dad and I always dreamed of going to Nashville someday and 'making music,' like he called it. He taught me how to play the guitar, and we sang together wherever we could, at churches and fairs in our county.

"We became known a little, and I started to believe my dream might actually happen. But then doctors diagnosed my dad with pancreatic cancer. He died less than four months after he got sick."

My throat tightens, and I shift on the couch. Without taking her eyes off Macy, Grace reaches over and takes my hand.

"Anyway," Macy continues her story. "I'd been at the new school two weeks, and it wasn't anything like I'd been expecting. The kids, especially the girls, were cliquey and unfriendly. A couple of the guys talked to me a few times, but the girls gave them a hard time, so they stopped."

Macy sits up a little straighter, and I sense we're getting to the real story.

"There was a talent contest," Macy whispers.

We all lean closer to hear better.

"Mom and I thought," her words sound stronger, "if I sang one of my songs in the contest, people would get to know me more, and maybe I could make some friends that way." Her smile is sad. "I actually won the contest, and at first, I did make new friends. But some girls were jealous and started making fun of me. They said I sounded like Mickey Mouse, so they started calling me Macy Mouse."

She glances at me. "I'm sorry, Jess, for running away last week. There's no way you could have known. The name got shortened to Mouse, and that's what everyone started calling me. I hated it!" Her voice trembles now.

My eyes burn. I remember the awful look on her face last week when I said, 'Mouse.' That explains a lot.

"Later, the bullying moved to the internet, and they posted pictures of mice on my Facebook page. They even had someone make a meme of me, caught in a mousetrap. Then they discussed what kind of special poison it would take to kill Macy Mouse."

These last words are whispered. Macy glances down, and I see tears dripping onto her jeans. Beside me, Grace sniffs and squeezes my hand tighter.

"Mom and I kept hoping they'd get bored and stop, but it didn't happen. The few friends I did have seemed scared to hang out with me anymore, so I was completely alone. We tried talking to the administrators, but the girl's parents are huge supporters of the school. Whatever the principal told them made them mad, and the bullying got worse.

"When the school year ended, most of them left for summer break, and the bullying stopped. I hoped when school began in August, I could start over. But that didn't happen."

Macy nods her thanks as Anna hands her a bottle of cold water.

She takes a sip, then continues, "On the second day of school, someone set a mousetrap in my locker. I reached in for my book, and the trap almost broke my finger. The online bullying started again, but this time the older girls made it an initiation for incoming freshmen girls. They could earn points for every post they made. Someone told me they could even earn bonus points if they made me cry."

Macy's determined expression impresses me, and I recalculate my earlier judgment of her. This girl has grit.

"I cried every night at home, but I never cried in front of them. Not once. I didn't tell Mom the bullying had started again because she was so busy with her job, and I didn't want to worry her. So, I tried to tough things out on my own. Until I couldn't." She takes a deep breath.

I've been holding my breath, too.

"Two weeks ago, I was in the cafeteria, eating lunch alone. I left the table to get a drink, and when I got back, someone had put a box of rat poison beside my plate."

I hear a low growl and glance at Cole, who appears ready to explode. Others in the group are having similar reactions. Several girls are crying now, and Pastor Jarrod paces in the doorway to the kitchen, his fists tightly clenched.

"Everyone started laughing and clapping like it was the funniest joke they'd ever seen. I refused to give them the satisfaction of seeing me break down. I simply picked up my book bag and walked out. I never went back." Macy leans against the wall with a sigh. "When Mom came home from work that night, I told her everything.

"She was heartbroken. She called Uncle John, and two days later, I was on a plane to Montana. Mom is flying out this weekend for a job interview in Dillon. I hope she gets it because I want to stay in Montana. And I want to be a part of this group, if you'll have me." She says the last words in a soft, wavering voice.

I'm amazed at Macy's courage in sharing such a deep hurt.

There's an explosion of movement as several girls surround Macy and hug her. Many are weeping in compassion.

"Macy," Kellen speaks up. "I experienced something similar when I was in junior high, and I can tell you, toughing it out on your own isn't the answer. As you learn to trust us more, you'll find out we've got your back. Always."

Tears fill Macy's eyes as she glances around, seeing the resolution on each face.

"Thank you. And I hope to be that kind of friend, too."

Pastor Jarrod stands and holds up his hands for attention. "Okay, BoB-ites. We're going to have a Bible scavenger hunt."

A chorus of cheers mixes with groans as everyone digs in purses and backpacks to find their Bibles.

Pastor Jarrod counts heads. "We're pretty evenly divided with guys and girls tonight, so those are the teams. Guys versus girls."

Todd snickers. "Versus or verses?"

Everyone groans.

"Bad puns will cost you one point each," Pastor Jarrod says.

"Totally worth it." Todd grins.

"Everyone have your Bible ready?" Pastor Jarrod asks. "The subject is words: how they help or how they hurt." He raises his left arm and points to his watch. "You have fifteen minutes. And go."

The sound of turning pages fills the room as everyone races to find a verse that fits the theme. I turn to Proverbs and speed read, looking for possible scriptures. It never fails when Pastor Jarrod announces a Bible scavenger hunt that my mind goes blank.

Imagining I can hear the ticking of Pastor Jarrod's watch, I manage to find a few verses that should give the girls' team a point.

Pastor Jarrod steps into the middle of the room. "Let's be gentlemen and start with the ladies. Who has a verse?"

Terri raises her hand, and Pastor Jarrod gives her a nod.

"'It is foolish to belittle a neighbor, a person with good sense remains silent' Proverbs 11:12 (NLT)," she reads.

"Excellent. In other words, if you can't say anything good ..." Pastor Jarrod holds up his hands, gesturing for us to finish the line.

We respond with a chorus of, "Don't say anything at all."

"Right. Okay, guys, you're up."

"Telling lies about others is as harmful as hitting them with an ax, wounding them with a sword, or shooting them with a sharp arrow. Proverbs 25:18 (NLT)," Kellen reads.

"Ouch," Pastor Jarrod says. "Don't mince words, Solomon, tell us what you really think."

Grace raises her hand. "I have one for the girls' team. Proverbs 16:24, 'Kind words are like honey, sweet to the soul, and healthy for the body' (NLT)."

More hands go up, and for the next few minutes, we take turns reading several verses.

"'Gentle words bring life and health, a deceitful tongue crushes the spirit' Proverbs 15:4 (NLT)."

"'A gentle answer turns away wrath, but harsh words stir up anger' Proverbs 15:1 (NLT)."

"'Evil words destroy one's friends, wise discernment rescues the Godly' Proverbs 11:9 (NLT)."

"'Your own soul is nourished when you are kind, but you destroy yourself when you are cruel' Proverbs 11:17 (NLT)," I read.

"'Words satisfy the soul as food satisfies the stomach; the right words on a person's lips bring satisfaction' Proverbs 18:20 (NLT),'" Todd reads.

"Of course, Todd finds the verse with food in it," Terri snickers.

"Okay, we're tied, four to four," Pastor Jarrod says. "Let's make the tiebreaker a hard one. I want a verse that's not in the Old Testament."

Cole stands. "1 Peter 3:10, 'If you want to enjoy life and see many happy days, keep your tongue from speaking evil and your lips from telling lies (NLT),'" he reads, then looks right at me.

"Uh oh," Grace mutters, "he knows."

"Knows what?" I ask, innocently. I put my Bible back in my bag as everyone congratulates the guys on the win.

She gives me her patented are-you-kidding-me look. "That you haven't told the entire story about what happened with Mark."

"Shh," I say, looking around to see if anyone is listening.

They aren't. Everyone gathers in the kitchen, sampling Mrs. Mendelsohn's latest creation: egg roll cookies. She'd delivered an enormous plate of the cookies this afternoon, and I generously decided to share them with the BoB group.

Okay, I wasn't being generous. Mrs. M had heard about egg roll cookies, but rather than making regular cookies in the shape of egg rolls, she made the cookies with actual egg roll ingredients.

"Don't worry, we can make popcorn," Anna calls from the kitchen.

I guess I'm not the only one who thinks cabbage and cookies don't make a delicious combo.

"I'll take the cookies home if no one wants them," Todd volunteers.

Todd eats anything.

Grace and I start to make a discreet exit when Cole walks into the living room.

He holds a can of Coke in one hand and a cookie in the other. I start to yell, *Don't eat that!* when I see him drop it into the nearby waste can. Wise choice.

"Jess, would you ride home with me? I'd like to talk to you."

I frantically look at Grace to rescue me.

"That's a great idea," she says. "I have a trig test tomorrow, and I need to study."

Then she's gone—the traitor.

12

Wednesday, September 12
9:00 p.m.

"Wow, Macy's story was unreal, right?" I chatter like a chipmunk as I ride next to Cole. "I mean, how cruel can people be? I'm sorry that happened to her, but at least we'll become part of her life now. BoB has needed more girls for a long time, ever since the Stuber girls moved back to Illinois."

Cole nods but says nothing.

"And what about the cookies Mrs. M sent?" I talk faster. "Egg roll cookies. I can't believe Todd ate so many and took the rest home. I hope Mrs. M doesn't enter them in a contest based on Todd's cookie consumption because we all know he'll eat anything, right?"

"Jess," Cole interrupts.

I ignore him and keep going. "I forgot we have a trig test tomorrow. I should have an extra day because I was out on Monday and missed one of the review days." No! I mentioned missing school on Monday. That will make Cole think of the accident, which is precisely the topic I'm avoiding.

Grace is the only person who is aware of what Mark planned

that night, and I merely told her part of the story. I want to keep it that way. Ugh. I would never make a good spy. I'd spill all our country's secrets by the end of the first day.

"Jess." Cole pulls into the parking lot of the First Baptist Church and turns off the engine. He looks at me with concern.

My face flushes, and I turn away, gazing out my window. I take several deep breaths, capturing my racing thoughts.

"Jess? Are you okay?"

I sense Cole studying me, and I wave my hand dismissively. "Of course," I say with feigned indifference. "I'm fine. Everything is fine."

Cole raises an eyebrow and objects, "Well, I'm fairly sure that isn't the case since your sister was arrested, and you were in a car accident. Not such a *fine* week, right?"

"No," I agree, shaking my head. "Not my finest."

Cole lifts his ball cap, running his hands through his dark hair, and then replaces the cap. That's a sure sign he's getting frustrated. "Well, I wanted to take you home because I need to ask you a question."

He sounds serious, and I brace myself for his questions concerning Mark and the accident.

Instead, he reaches for my hand. "Jess, would you go to Homecoming with me?" he asks in a rush.

"I ... umm ... what?" I've been so focused on what I'll say about Mark, I can't process Cole's words. My mouth hangs open, which is not an attractive look for me. I snap it closed.

"Homecoming?" He raises his eyebrows. "You remember, that dance the school has every year around this time? You get dressed up a lot, and I get dressed up a little. We have dinner with some friends and then go to the dance. Homecoming." His mouth quirks with his teasing.

I laugh. "Oh, *that* Homecoming. Yes. I mean, yes, as in I understand what you're talking about." I add stupidly, "I like Homecoming."

He grins. "I like Homecoming, too. And I'll like it even more if you go with me."

His face shows amusement, but his eyes hold an unmistakable seriousness that makes me feel a little melty inside. Cole gently runs his thumb over the top of my hand.

"Jessica Ann Thomas, will you go to Homecoming with me? I'm sorry I'm not asking you with any special effects, like when Todd asked Hannah last week. I mean, who can top that?"

I remember the invitation Todd persuaded Pastor Jeff to post on the church sign. It was up for less than an hour before Hannah drove by, saw it, and accepted immediately. Hannah loved the idea, but I'd have been super embarrassed.

"No," I say, shaking my head at the thought.

For a minute, Cole appears surprised, then hurt. "That's okay." His tone is gruff as he turns the truck ignition.

"Cole, wait." I grasp his flannel covered arm.

He shakes his head, and with a light shrug of his shoulders, shifts the truck into drive. "It's okay, Jess." His tone turns casual. "I get you have a lot going on right now. And I guess I misunderstood what I thought is happening between us. It really is okay." With his gaze straight ahead, foot on the gas, he eases us across the open lot.

"Cole Dougal McBride," I jab the tight muscle of his upper arm. If he can use all my names, I can use all his.

That gets his attention. Cole hates his middle name. He brakes, and we both lurch forward.

"When I said no, I meant no—you don't need to ask in a special way. In fact, you asked just right." I smile and teasingly rub the spot on his arm where I'd poked him. "And yes, I will go to Homecoming with you."

The vulnerability on his face takes me by surprise. He hasn't asked me to Homecoming to be nice—he actually *wants* this date. I try to appear calm, but inside, I'm twirling around like a little girl.

Cole switches off the ignition and turns to face me. "Jess." He leans close.

I hold my breath. Is he going to kiss me?

Whoop, whoop. We jump apart as Deputy Nick drives by with a salute and a grin. We groan.

"Does he have a tracker on your truck or something?" I grumble.

"I'm not sure." Cole grimaces as he turns to put the truck in gear. "But I'm definitely going to discuss his timing."

Saturday, September 15
11:00 a.m.

"THIS FEELS WRONG." I tug at the lace scratching my neck.

"It looks great," Grace says. "This color definitely highlights the green in your eyes."

"No, not the dress, although, for the record, I hate lace. I mean, it's wrong to be out shopping when we don't know what will happen to Sly. It's been a whole week, and we're still in the dark." Turning around, I motion for Grace to unzip me.

Sly walks into the large dressing area carrying more torture devices—aka, dresses—for me to model.

"Jess, stop worrying and enjoy the day." She lays the dresses on a nearby bench.

"If you want me to enjoy the day, why are we shopping?" I whisper as Grace helps me slip out of the green dress.

Sly holds up a gauzy yellow and pink dress.

I shake my head, muttering, "I'd look like a cupcake."

"Did you say something?" Sly asks.

Maggie rushes into the dressing area, carrying an assortment of clutches.

"I like this one," Maggie holds up a truly ugly purse covered in embroidered cats.

Grace and I exchange grins as Sly diplomatically explains that cats might not be appropriate for the homecoming dance. When Maggie questions this decision, Sly reminds her that our school mascot is a bulldog. Maggie appears to accept this logic and leaves the room to return the purse.

"Dodged that bullet," Sly mumbles as she lifts a deep crimson dress from the pile.

It shocks me to realize I don't hate it. I reach out to touch the soft, velvet fabric, which is surprisingly lightweight. It has what Grace describes as a sweetheart neckline and short cap sleeves with a small ruffle. I'm delighted the full skirt has tiny, hidden pockets in the side. The room quiets as I slip the dress over my head, and it settles down to skim above my knees.

"Perfect," Grace whispers.

I spin, and the skirt swirls around my knees. "I like it." But what I actually mean is, I love it. I'm not a huge fan of dresses, but this one makes me feel special like it's been made exactly for me.

I glance at Sly, surprised to see tears shimmering in her eyes.

"Hey." I step toward my sister. "What's wrong?"

She brushes the tears away. "You look so much like Mamma in that dress. She would've loved to be with us today."

My throat tightens, and I hug her, stepping away before I completely break down. I don't want Maggie to come in and see us crying.

In the end, we buy the velvet dress for me and the cat purse for Maggie, since she loves it. The fact we're shopping in Bozeman at Twice Treasured Thrift, which raises money for a local Christian school, makes it easy on our budget.

We drive back to Justice and finish the afternoon with a stop at The Dairy Barn, then drop Grace off at the Ellison's. I'm guiltily glad she'll be babysitting all night because she definitely wouldn't approve of my plans for the evening.

Saturday, September 15
5:15 p.m.

I PARK my bike near the edge of the woods and sneak toward the building site. It's nearly dark, and I need to hurry if I hope to find anything tonight. Removing a small flashlight from my backpack, I gingerly step over a concrete slab blocking my way.

Sliding the phone from my pocket, I touch the camera setting and take aim at a partially finished brick wall. If Robert fired Sly because of her pictures, maybe I'll find something suspicious. Since I'm not sure what I'm looking for, I point and click, taking random shots.

I spend several minutes documenting the materials lying around and then focus on the construction.

Glancing up, I notice an elevator attached to the building. The workers must use it to move between levels. I look around, and confident I'm alone, I scramble over some bricks and climb into the elevator. I study the controls for a moment and press *up*. Nothing happens. Well, duh.

The workers turned off the generator that powers the site. There's no way up, except, of course, the old-fashioned way.

A few months earlier, Cole invited me to Timber Ridge, a rock-climbing club. I learned a few basics that day, and now I put the training to use. Grabbing a nearby paint bucket to stand on, I climb the outside of the elevator. Now I remember why I never returned to the climbing wall with Cole. Vertigo.

I heave myself onto the roof of the elevator, my head and stomach swirling. A glance over the side shows I'm even with the second floor of the unfinished building. I remove my phone, taking some shots of the unfinished walls with their bright yellow insulation. Next, I point toward the back of the building and snap a few more photos.

From my vantage point, I can tell I've captured most of the different angles. Now I have to find a way down from here.

Easier said than done. Grabbing the top edge of the elevator, I slowly lower myself over the side. The elevator shakes a little, and I hold tighter to the edge. I can't stay in this position long since I'm visible to anyone who cares to look.

Reaching for the next ledge with my toe, I tentatively settle, feeling more secure. Until I'm not. My foot slips, and I frantically grab for something, anything, that will keep me connected to the elevator. Both feet dangle in midair, and I can hear my heart drumming as I grapple for a secure handhold.

Fingers tightening around a small beam, I hold on for dear life. My backpack tugs my shoulders as I hang, balancing between the first and second story. I could take my chances and drop—it's approximately eight feet. But piles of bricks and concrete cover the ground under my feet—not exactly the soft landing I prefer.

My fingers slipping, I glance down, judging where I can aim that might cause the fewest injuries. Vertigo hits me again, and I grasp the railing tighter.

This is *so* not good.

"Please, God. Please, God," I pray, trying to get a toehold, my stomach roiling with nausea. My Keds touch a solid surface but slip off and dangle in midair. Arms screaming with pain, I picture myself falling through the air, onto the concrete blocks.

"Please, God."

Calm settles over me, and the tension in my shoulders eases a bit. Extending my foot, I touch a hard surface. There! Concentrating, I slide the tip of my shoe into a more secure position on the metal bar. I balance there on the toe of my shoe, then gently swing my dangling foot to touch the rebar.

The bottom of the elevator hangs a few feet from the ground, and I drop, landing on the blocks. My feet tingle from the impact, but finally, I'm standing on solid ground again.

"Ladies and gentlemen, Jessica Thomas has stuck the landing," I mutter the words, scrambling over the concrete blocks, and race to my bike. It's dark, and I still have to get home before Sly realizes I'm gone. Riding through the quiet streets of Justice, I pray I've found enough evidence to prove Sly's innocence.

I slip through the kitchen door and head to the fridge for a cold water bottle.

"Hey, Jess. Where have you been?" Sly startles me as she gently hip-nudges me away, and rummaging through the refrigerator, grabs a yogurt container.

"Oh, hanging out," I mumble, pushing down my guilt. Brushing by her, I climb the stairs to my room and go straight to my computer. I open my phone's camera app and upload the pictures to my laptop. The photos splay out in front of me, and I realize I have a problem. I have no idea what I'm seeing.

Disappointment settles over me. My photos show various equipment and parts of the completed building, but to my eye, everything looks normal. Sly must have taken pictures of something she wasn't supposed to see, but these photos are worthless. Whatever she saw caused Robert Sinclair to panic and fire her. The answer must be on Sly's camera. Now I need to find it.

13

I admit my mind wanders during the sermon on Sunday. The part I do hear sounds like an exciting story about a woman named Jael, who delivered the Israelites from an evil king and his army. I pick up the phrase 'tent peg in his temple' and decide I'll read Jael's story for myself later.

The McBrides invited us for Sunday dinner, and my stomach rumbles. Sly nudges me in the ribs, but what can I do? Mrs. McBride has promised lasagna, and I hope she'll also serve homemade bread and some variety of pie. Lemon, maybe. Or chocolate. My stomach growls again, and Sly frowns.

The sermon ends at that moment, and the growls are drowned when the worship band leads the last song. We make our way to the exit, saying hello to several people. Mrs. Hanover stops Sly and gives her a tight hug.

"I'm praying for you, sweetie," she says. Mrs. Hanover is around one hundred years old and wears tons of perfume, but she's very sweet. Sly takes a deep breath before she leans closer to return the hug.

"Thank you, Mrs. Hanover. I'm so grateful for your prayers." Sly starts to turn a little red from lack of oxygen.

I take my own deep breath and step closer to distract Mrs. Hanover so Sly doesn't pass out.

"You look pretty today, Mrs. Hanover," I say. She might be old, but her smooth complexion has few wrinkles. I should look so good at her age.

"Thank you, dear," she says. "Jess, are you okay? You seem flushed."

I release the breath I'm holding and start to answer, but Sly steps in for her turn. Sly and I have done this choreographed dance with Mrs. Hanover for years. We have it down to an art form.

"I think Jess is hungry," Sly responds. "The McBrides are expecting us for Sunday dinner."

At the name McBride, Mrs. Hanover's bright blue eyes turn stormy. "Well, I'm not sure you should eat at the table of your enemy," she states bluntly.

Sly appears startled by this statement. "I'm not sure what you mean?"

"Why, I mean Nicholas McBride is the one who arrested you!" Mrs. Hanover says with genuine anger. "I can't believe he did such a thing. I am extremely disappointed in that young man."

Sly's face turns red, but I suspect it isn't because of Mrs. Hanover's perfume.

"Mrs. Hanover," Sly says, obviously working hard to be respectful. "Nick is kind and professional, and I have no problem with my treatment by the Sheriff's department. This is a terrible mistake, and I'm sure it will be resolved soon."

For a minute, Mrs. Hanover appears surprised by Sly's firm response. Then she gives a slow smile and says, "So, it's like that, is it?"

Sly flushes while I try to figure out what Mrs. Hanover means. What is 'like that'?

Mrs. Hanover pats Sly's arm. "Good for you, my dear. Nicholas deserves a strong woman who will stand up for him. Enjoy your family dinner, girls." Then she's gone, her perfume wafting after her.

Sly rummages through her purse, probably searching for her keys.

"What did she mean?" I ask.

"I have no idea. Let's go. I'm starved." Her face glows bright red.

And once again, I doubt it's from holding her breath to avoid the perfume.

Sunday, September 16
12:30 p.m.

SUNDAY DINNER at the McBrides is always an event. Nick and Cole's older sister, Piper, and her husband, Jack, will be there, along with their four-year-old daughter, Merri. That name suits her, too. Merri is the happiest little girl I've ever met. I'm looking forward to the afternoon with Cole's family.

Sly drops Maggie and me at home, so we can change out of our church clothes. Sly is hurrying because she wants to help Mrs. McBride get dinner ready. I think she wants to keep wearing the pink sweater dress and pearls she wore to church. She has on cream-colored half-boots, and her hair is spiked in perfect symmetry.

As she drives away, it occurs to me that Sly hasn't dressed up like that in a long time. Interesting.

I race to my room and grab my jeans off the floor, where I store them. I change from my navy skirt and reach for Daddy's old Montana University sweatshirt. Glimpsing myself in the dresser mirror, I decide I prefer the heather gray sweater I'm wearing. It goes well with the jeans. I'll need to be super careful and not drip lasagna on the front.

Maggie meets me in the hallway. She's also changed into jeans and one of Sly's old college T-shirts. She seems to be anticipating lots of outdoor fun with Merri and Roxie today.

We make the five-minute walk in three-and-a-half. I'm torn between hurrying to get my share of lasagna and studying the variegated colors of the trees. Down the street, someone is burning leaves, and I inhale the scent. There's nothing quite like the smell of smoke on a crisp fall afternoon.

I put my arm around Maggie's shoulder. "Hey, Magpie, I've barely seen you this week. How's it going?"

"Great," Maggie says.

I hope that's true. The sounds of Roxie barking and Merri laughing interrupt us as we approach the McBride home. Everyone, except Mrs. McBride, Piper, and Sly, is in the front yard playing Frisbee. Maggie races to join them, and I smile when I hear her excited laughter. There have been no nightmares for several days, and I pray we've weathered that storm for now.

Dinner tastes delicious as expected. Mrs. McBride has outdone herself with not one, not two, but three pies: lemon, chocolate, and strawberry rhubarb. While we eat, we avoid discussing Sly's arrest, and it feels nice to relax and have fun. Tension eases, and I feel wrapped in a cocoon of peace.

After dinner, the McBride family has an interesting tradition. Anyone who helped prepare the food is exempt from cleanup. Mrs. McBride, Piper, and Sly take Merri to the living room to play Candyland. Maggie watches them with longing, and I give her a gentle push.

"Go on, Magpie, I'll work doubly hard for you."

She gives me a quick hug and calls, "Hey, wait for me," as she runs to the living room.

Even though they have a large kitchen, I feel dwarfed between Cole, Nick, and Jack. Mr. McBride assigns himself the job of 'securing the dessert leftovers,' and carries the pies into the small breakfast nook. Nick and Cole keep glancing in that direction, obviously worried their dad believes the most secure place for the dessert is in his stomach.

Nick scrapes the plates, Cole washes, and I dry. Jack is the designated fridge organizer since, apparently, he has OCD. We make a good team, and in less than twenty minutes, the kitchen gleams. As Cole and I leave the room, he glances out the kitchen window and stops in his tracks. Of course, I run into him.

"Hey," I oomph. Cole is not a small guy.

He doesn't answer but nods his head toward the window.

I follow his gaze and notice Nick and Sly talking under the rose arbor. Nick is tall, and Sly appears petite beside him. They are standing very close to each other, and Nick lowers his head.

"They must be plotting strategy to expose Robert Sinclair," I say.

But instead of whispering in Sly's ear, Nick leans closer and kisses her. And not a friend comforting a friend kiss. A second later, she steps closer, looping her arms around his neck, and returns the kiss.

My mouth drops open.

"That looks like a great strategy to me." Cole grins and nudges me toward the living room. "C'mon. We're missing Candyland."

14

Sunday, September 16
8:00 p.m.

"Jessica Ann Thomas, this is the stupidest thing you've ever done," I whisper the words as Cole's pickup hits a bump, and I nearly smack my head on the bed of the truck. Minutes earlier, I'd slipped into the back of the pickup, covering myself with a paint tarp I'd found.

Now I wrinkle my nose. Has Cole been hauling manure? My Eden Spring shampoo will remove the odor from my hair. Maybe I'll trash my clothes later.

Cole hits another bump, and I wonder if he's aware I'm hiding back here and is purposely taking me over the roughest roads. After the Candyland game, Cole received a text from Robert Sinclair. Chieftain was stabled at Robert's house for the weekend and needed Cole's attention.

When I heard where he was going, I realized this might be my only chance to find Sly's camera. It's a longshot because Robert might have already destroyed it. But hopefully, while Robert and Cole are talking in the stable, I can sneak into Robert's office. Maybe the camera is hidden there.

Just when I think my ribs have been jarred loose, Cole slows the pickup, and I lift the tarp for a peek. Large outdoor lights illuminate the parking area around the stable, and I hold my breath as Cole slams the truck door and crunches across the rocks. A moment later, Cole opens the door to the stable, and Robert's voice calls from inside.

It's now or never. For a second, I consider *never* as an option. Then I remember Maggie's face the night before when she worried we'd live with strangers if Sly went to jail. That will not happen.

I slide from my hiding spot, keeping to the shadows. Glancing over my shoulder, I slip through the front door and head for the office. I was there once with Cole when he delivered medicine for Chieftain. Now, I rush to Robert's desk. Locked.

Of course, it's locked. Duh. I run my fingers under the desk drawer, and I'm rewarded with a splinter. Sucking my finger, I wander around the room, searching for a possible hiding spot for the camera.

A metal file cabinet sits in the corner, and I tug on the top drawer. Locked. This is becoming a pattern. I start to turn away, but moonlight reflects the glint of something shiny. A key is tucked under the edge of a potted plant. Grabbing the key, I turn it in the cabinet's lock. Success.

I yank open the first drawer and discover that it's filled with … files. Right. Filing cabinet. Files. So predictable. I tug on the second drawer and find more files. The third drawer appears only partially full, though, so I reach into the space, feeling for the camera. No luck.

Removing my hand from the drawer, I glance at the files and notice one labeled Thomas. The file feels thick, and I hesitate. There might be information on Sly, but there's no time to look. My heart pounds as I slide the entire file into my backpack.

My conscience nags me. It's one thing to take Sly's camera, but something else entirely to steal a file. I bite my lip and justify my action. My family name is on the folder. That kind of makes it mine, right?

Moving away from the cabinet, I scan the room. There's a closet in a corner, and I open the louvered door, revealing shelves stacked with boxes and books. Robert is frighteningly neat. I consider that fact alone makes him a suspect. There's neat, and then there's obsessive.

I start to close the door and notice three books aren't perfectly aligned with the others.

Sloppy, Robert. Pulling out the three volumes of Shakespeare, I lean down and investigate. Sly's camera nestles in the open space. Chills run up my spine as I realize what this means. Robert stole Sly's camera, which means he lied about Sly stealing the money.

But why? And if something incriminating is on the camera, why didn't he destroy it? All good questions for later.

I grab the camera and drop it into my backpack, carefully replacing the books. Then I jump a little when I hear voices in the hallway. Robert and Cole are coming toward the office.

Squeezing into the closet, I close the door as they enter the room. I consider holding my breath but decide with my luck, I'll probably pass out and fall at their feet. Instead, I concentrate on slowing my breathing and attempt to stay motionless.

"Thanks for delivering the medicine for Chieftain's hoof," Robert says. Through the slats of the door, I see him cross to the desk, pulling a key from his pocket.

"Happy to help," Cole responds. "I hope that does the trick." There's the distinctive sound of paper being torn, and I peek through the louvered doors to see Robert handing Cole a check.

"I'll stop back tomorrow after class," Cole says. He folds the check and slides it into his jean's pocket. "When Ben returns from vacation, he'll let you know if Chieftain needs more treatment. I think we caught the problem in time, but if not, Ben will take care of it."

They leave the office, and a few seconds later, the front door clicks closed behind them. I peek out of the closet, relieved to see the empty foyer. I have to hurry.

Exiting through the patio door, I see Cole and Robert walking toward the stable. Good. I'll climb into the truck bed and pull that smelly tarp over me again before Cole leaves. I start to sprint when Robert stops and motions toward the pickup.

"Cole, you don't need to spend any more of your time here." Robert's voice floats in the quiet night. "I'll watch Chieftain until he settles down."

I stop mid-sprint and examine my options. I'm completely exposed here in the driveway, with the outside lights practically flashing my location. If Cole turns around, he'll spot me, and I can't think of any plausible reason for my sudden appearance. I can't say I was out walking and ended up in the neighborhood. We're five miles from town.

The exact second that Cole turns to leave, I race toward the woods flanking the other side of the driveway. Praying my dark clothes disguise me, I melt into the trees as the truck engine starts. Whew, Cole hasn't seen me. I sincerely pray that nothing shares my new hiding spot. At least nothing with teeth.

My thoughts race as I gasp for breath. I'm hiding in the woods, five miles from civilization, and my ride is speedily disappearing. I certainly can't knock on Robert Sinclair's door and ask for a ride home. Uber? I push down a hysterical laugh.

No, my sole choice is walking through the woods until there's no chance Robert can see me. Then I'll try to locate a cell signal and call Grace. Maybe she can ask her parents for permission to drive to Walmart. Then she can pick me up and take me home. Great, now I'm making my friend an accomplice.

A rustling sound startles me, and I frantically look around to see who, or what, has joined me. I'm not sure if I prefer Robert Sinclair or a bear. Moonlight gives me a quick glimpse of a doe standing ten feet away. We probably wear matching looks of surprise.

We stare at each other for a second, then turn in opposite directions and run. I promptly charge into a huge spiderweb that wraps around my entire face. Swatting at the silky strands, I pray the spider is on vacation.

A deep shudder runs through me, partly from the cold, but mostly because I hate spiders. A lot. My pounding heart slows, and I continue my trek through the woods, relieved when I finally reach the highway. A few cars drive by, but I draw the line at hitchhiking. There's stupid, and then there's insane.

I estimate I've walked a half-mile when a vehicle approaches from the opposite direction. I step into the shadows, hoping to avoid the headlights. But the driver must notice me because the truck slows and then stops right next to my hiding spot. I squint in the darkness. Then my breath hitches as I recognize my good Samaritan.

Cole.

He pulls the truck closer, and the automatic window lowers to release a waft of warm air. "You might as well get in."

I can't tell his mood from the tone in his voice, but at that point, I don't care. I'm tired, cold, covered in web, and pretty sure I'm being stalked by a pack of wolves. I ungraciously yank open the door and climb into the cab. Without a word, Cole swings the truck around and heads back toward Justice.

The silence lasts for a few minutes, and I spend time warming my hands near the heater vent.

"How?" I finally ask.

He glances over at me. "Eden Spring." He gives a cryptic answer.

"Huh?"

"Your shampoo or perfume, or whatever. I asked you one time what it is, and you said Eden Spring. When I walked into Robert's office, I caught a whiff and figured you had to be somewhere close. When I was out of sight of the ranch, I stopped and checked the truck bed. It has the same smell."

I grin despite the situation. "It's a miracle you smelled anything other than the manure stink back there."

Cole frowns, obviously ready for some serious conversation. "What were you thinking? You snuck into my truck, then hid in Robert Sinclair's office. For what? I get that you don't trust him, but what were you hoping to accomplish?"

Apparently, he's just getting warmed up.

"What if I hadn't gone into Robert's office or recognized your perfume?"

"Shampoo," I mutter.

"What?"

"Not perfume, shampoo."

"Whatever!" Cole is rapidly losing patience. "You could have been stuck up here on the mountain, and no one would know where you were. Did you plan to walk the five miles to Justice? In the dark?" His voice has risen with each word.

"I planned to call Grace," I say sullenly. I hate it when Cole's right. It was dangerous and stupid, and I'm fortunate to be sitting in his warm truck right now. Instead, I could be playing hide-and-seek in the woods with coyotes, and wolves, and bears. I manage to contain a giggle, thinking of the line from *The Wizard of Oz*—Lions, and tigers, and bears, oh, my!

He glares at me. "Do you think this is funny?"

I stare hard at him. He isn't merely angry. He's scared. For me. I'm understanding the situation from his perspective and slowly reach out and touch his arm.

"I honestly am sorry, Cole. You're right, I wasn't thinking, and this could have ended very badly. I'm sorry." I repeat.

He gives me a suspicious glance, probably trying to determine if I'm sincere. He must decide yes, because after a moment, his face softens, and he reaches out to squeeze my hand.

"Jess."

I give his hand a quick squeeze in return, and my throat

seems tight like I might cry. I swallow and glance away, the moment broken.

"So, what did you find?" He asks in a calmer voice.

I look at him, startled. "How do you know I found anything?"

He shrugs. "I'm not sure." He sounds genuinely surprised at himself. "I guess I can read you pretty well, and I don't think you're shivering from the cold. You're excited. Right?"

I reach into my backpack and pull out Sly's camera. "Oh yeah, I found something."

15

Sunday, September 16
10:00 p.m.

I wrap my hands around the steaming mug of hot chocolate Sly prepared for me. The heat from the cup warms my still-frozen fingers. Across the table, Cole sips his own chocolate, and I can sense him watching me. Now comes the moment of truth. We're going to discover if there is anything incriminating on Sly's camera.

Sly places her laptop on the table, pulls the SD card from the camera, and plugs it into the slot. A few clicks of the mouse, and the screen fills with dozens of pictures. For a minute, I feel a little deflated. These are boring pictures of a building under construction, not much different from the ones I took. I'm not sure what I expected to see. She hasn't taken a picture of an actual crime being committed.

Sly scrolls through the images as Cole stands to look over my shoulder.

"That one." He points at the screen. "Stop there, Sly."

She enlarges the picture Cole indicated, and the screen

shows an image of Robert Sinclair and ... who? I squint and lean in for a better view.

"Who is that?" I mutter.

"Not a clue," Cole replies.

Sly is quiet for a moment, then says, "There's something familiar about him."

"Care to share with the class?"

Jumping at the unexpected voice, I glance up. Nick stands in the kitchen doorway. He's wearing his Deputy's uniform, and my pulse increases as I realize I might have, possibly, maybe, broken the law tonight. Just a tiny bit. Why couldn't Cole's brother be an accountant or something?

Nick moves to Sly's side and casually places his arm around her shoulder. I file that under weird but interesting stuff to think about later.

"Well," says Cole, "if they're doing something wrong, why are they doing it in front of witnesses. Wouldn't they try to hide the connection?"

"I think I understand what happened," Sly says slowly. "I was chronicling the placement of the beams, and I moved alongside the building for a better shot. Since I focused on what I was doing, I didn't pay attention to the two men. I remember Robert looked up and saw me with the camera. Maybe he thinks I was spying on him or something. I would have edited them out of the shot that weekend if he hadn't fired me and taken my camera."

She sits back, and I notice Nick is gently rubbing Sly's shoulders, consoling her. The weird but interesting file keeps getting larger.

"Well, here's a question." Cole walks to the sink to rinse his mug. "If Robert Sinclair is so afraid of what's on the camera, why didn't he destroy the evidence instead of hiding it?"

"Exactly," I say. "I wondered the same thing."

"Sly, can I take the camera and SD card with me?" Nick asks.

She removes the SD card, placing it in the camera, and

hands it to him. "Of course. Although could I get it back, eventually? Mamma and Daddy gave me the camera for Christmas."

"I can make that happen," Nick assures her. Then he glances at me. "When this is all over, let's have a chat, hum?"

I glare at Cole. "You told him!"

He shrugs, "How was I going to explain where the camera came from? The Easter Bunny delivered it?"

"Wait," Sly says. "If the pictures are evidence, can you use them since there wasn't a warrant to search Robert's house?"

"Since Jess is a private citizen, and she's not representing the police, they should be admissible. But she may be in trouble for breaking and entering." Nick gives me a stern look.

I shrug. "I retrieved my sister's property," I state primly. "It's not like I'm going to Juvie."

Nick opens his mouth to say something but apparently reconsiders and shakes his head. "I'll take this to the Sheriff, and we'll see what we can discover concerning the relationship between Robert Sinclair and the mystery man." He leans toward Sly. "Walk me out?"

She nods, and as they leave the kitchen, Nick slips his arm around her shoulder.

I turn to catch Cole, watching his brother and my sister.

"Weird," he says.

I nod. "And interesting."

Monday, September 17
8:30 a.m.

I OPEN MY EYES, enjoying a brief moment of peace. The sun shines through my bedroom window, and I anticipate one of those amazing fall days I love so much. The best part, there's no school because of a teacher's institute. Grace, Maggie, and I will ride our bikes to the local apple orchard and then come home to bake pies.

Well, Sly will bake the pies since she's a great cook. I expect I'll spend the day peeling apples, but that's okay. The payoff will be amazing.

Slowly, though, reality seeps into my consciousness. Last night I found Sly's camera, and I need to know what Nick has discovered.

The delicious aroma of pancakes drifts up the stairs, and I literally follow my nose to the kitchen. Maggie is drawing designs on her chocolate chip pancakes, using maple syrup as paint. Yum. Sly hasn't made her famous breakfast in months, and I'm famished. I slip into my chair as Sly turns with another platter.

"Good morning," she smiles and slides three pancakes onto my plate. At my pleading gaze, she adds another.

I grab the syrup pitcher, then make a little syrup puddle at the edge of my plate. "Sly, these are amazing." I manage to speak the words clearly and still chew.

She shrugs, a little self-consciously, I think. A weight appears to have lifted from my sister. But it's more than that. Despite everything we've gone through these past weeks, Sly seems ... happy.

"What?" She stops with her fork half-way to her mouth. "Do I have butter on my nose or something?"

I give her an innocent smile. "No, you're gorgeous as usual." Her expression turns suspicious.

"What have you done now?"

"Nothing." For a minute, I consider being insulted, but decide it's too much effort. And besides, my pancakes will get cold. "You look ... glowy."

Maggie stops in mid-chew. "Glowy. Is that a word?"

"It is now," I say with a teasing grin at Sly. "It's a Sly word. In fact," I continue, watching a gentle blush creep up Sly's cheeks,

"I noticed a glow last night when you and Nick stood outside talking for twenty minutes."

"Wait," says Maggie. "Nick was here? And I missed him?" She stabs at a piece of pancake that apparently offends her.

"Yep," I say. "Cole was here, too."

Maggie stabs another bite, obviously disappointed all the fun stuff happened after she went to bed.

"How come they stopped by so late?" she asks around a mouthful of pancake.

I start to answer, but a sharp kick to my ankle makes me jump. "Ouch." I shoot a questioning glance at Sly, grateful she's wearing slippers instead of boots.

"They wanted to say hi." Sly answers Maggie's' question and gives me a meaningful look that says, *Keep this between us for now.*

I nod, glad Sly prevented me from telling Maggie about the camera. While it's probably good news, we can't take a chance she'll accidentally repeat something that will get back to Robert Sinclair. It's likely his involvement is criminal. We need to keep the information quiet until Nick solves the case.

"So, what's your plan for today?" Sly asks.

"Apples," we answer together.

Sly smiles, "Then I guess I need to find Gramma's recipe for pie crust and get ready."

Breakfast cleanup is a breeze as we all work together, and in a few minutes, Maggie and I pedal our bikes toward Grace's house.

Hydrangea bushes border the Compton home, which sits at the end of a long driveway. Grace's mom planted the small trees when they moved from Atlanta. Her mother felt uprooted from Georgia, and she wanted a reminder of their previous home. A wrap-around porch surrounds the two-story house, and several colorful rocking chairs are arranged to give a perfect view of the mountains.

I love Grace's home because I sense the love and warmth of the family living there. This was my safe, healing place during those terrible days after my parents died.

Maggie and I prop our bikes against the porch and climb the steps. But before we reach the top, Grace erupts through the front door. Before I can ask why she's in such a hurry, her older brother launches through the swinging screen door. Laughing, he fires foam darts from a Nerf gun, and several orange darts decorate Grace's long hair.

"Stop it!" she tries scowling through her laughter as she bats at the flying darts. "Matthew Carter Compton, I'm gonna' tell Mom if you don't stop right now!"

Matt releases one more dart, then spots Maggie standing on the porch steps. With a grin, he reloads and points at her.

"Run!" We all shriek as Matt chases Maggie through the front yard and around the side of the house.

"Watch out for Mom's flowers," Grace yells as the laughter drifts away.

She grabs my arm and tows me over to sit in the rocking chairs. "I got your very cryptic text. What happened last night?"

I describe hiding in Cole's truck and finding Sly's camera in Robert Sinclair's office.

Grace's eyes widen with each word, her expression a mixture of concern and pride. She wisely waits until I finish before she responds. She starts to speak, shaking her head as if rejecting that sentence, and tries again. Nope. Still no words.

Finally, Grace closes her eyes as if she's praying, then opens them. "Okay."

"Okay?" I ask. "That's all you have to say, okay?"

She stands so abruptly her chair rocks back against the porch railing. "What should I say?" she demands. "Great job finding the camera? Of course. But, Jess, what were you thinking? What if someone besides Cole found you on the highway? You could be halfway to Billings right now with some crazed serial killer! Or what if Robert discovered you with the camera after Cole left?"

Her soft southern drawl disappears, replaced with an angry tone. "Robert's not a good guy, Jess. He could have hurt you. No one knew you were there. Not even me. He could have made you disappear, and we would never know what happened to you."

Tears glimmer in Grace's eyes, and I'm on my feet, hugging my friend.

"Gracie, I'm so sorry. I didn't think about that. I didn't tell you because you'd try to stop me. Or you might have told Cole, who would definitely stop me. But please understand, I have to fix this." I swipe at my own tears.

"Why?" Her tone softens as she studies my face. "Why do *you* have to fix this?"

Shrugging away, I grab my bike. "I just do," I mutter. Then I swing my leg over the bike, turning to face her again.

"It isn't your fault," she says.

"Right," I answer. "It's Robert Sinclair's fault, and I'll make sure he pays for everything he's done to my family."

Grace shakes her head. "Jess, you know that's not what I mean."

I stiffen, not willing to respond. Instead, I say tightly, "I'm heading to the orchard. Will you ride along with Maggie, and I'll see you there?"

I sense her studying me as I pedal down the driveway. Grace knows me too well. I can't afford to forget that fact.

TIPTON'S ORCHARD and Pumpkin Patch is less than a mile from Grace's house. Even at 9:00 a.m., a dozen cars sit parked next to a large log cabin that serves as a café and gift shop. I climb the wooden steps, glancing down at a red wagon holding a display of small pumpkins, gourds, and sunflowers. Opening the door, I'm greeted by some of my favorite smells: cinnamon, apples, and sugar.

Tipton's is famous for their enormous cinnamon rolls, and I spend a blissful minute inhaling the scent. As I take my next breath, a wave of longing washes over me. The last time I came to Tipton's was with Mamma. High school had started a few weeks earlier, and it was a rough adjustment for me. Sly was attending her first year of college, and Grace hadn't moved to Justice yet.

Although I had some friends from church, they were homeschooled and didn't attend Justice High School. Many classmates were new to me since Justice draws students from neighboring areas. I was a little lost and a lot lonely.

One Saturday in September, Mamma had taken me to Tipton's. We'd had a wonderful morning, eating pumpkin bread, drinking hot cocoa, and talking. She was a wonderful listener, and by the time we left the cafe with a cinnamon roll for Daddy and some pumpkin-shaped cookies for Maggie, I felt better than I had in weeks.

I saw a poster once that said, *Sometimes, memories sneak out of my eyes and roll down my cheeks*. I understand exactly how that feels. In those first few months after my parents' deaths, I tried pushing down those loving memories because I hate tears. But eventually, I made a decision. I refuse to lose the only thing I have left of them. Now, I try leaning into the memories more, thankful for the precious time we had together.

Brushing away a stray tear, I cross the store, the wooden floor creaking under my feet. A pair of sunflower shaped salt and pepper shakers draws my attention.

"I thought I'd find you here." A voice whispers near my ear.

I jump, relieved I'd already set down the ceramic shakers, and turn to see Cole standing behind me. His black T-shirt reads, *Hold your horses*.

"Classy." I snicker and nod at the words.

He grins and reaches to tuck a stray lock of hair behind my ear. "C'mon. Grace and Maggie are waiting for us outside. Maggie wants to go through the corn maze before we pick apples."

I follow Cole outside into the bright sunlight. Grace and

Maggie stand beside a wagon attached to a small tractor. Several people sit on hay bales, waiting for a ride to the corn maze.

"Magpie, I'm not planning to spend the day here." I groan. "We're going to pick apples and get home so we can start on the pies."

"Please, Jess." Maggie's brown eyes take on that puppy dog look I can't resist.

"Okay, but you owe me, kiddo."

Maggie squeals and hugs me. Then, she runs and jumps on the back of the wagon, Grace in tow. Cole and I follow them, finding a semi-secure seat on the hay.

"We need to talk," Cole whispers as we bounce over the track leading to the maze. He nudges Grace, who sits on his other side. "Grace, maybe you and Maggie can team up for a contest? We'll see if you can get out of the maze before Jess and me."

The wagon pulls to a gentle stop, and Maggie hops off. "You're on." Grabbing Grace, she pulls her toward the maze.

Grace sends me a glance I interpret to mean, you-owe-me-big, and I nod.

Cole and I are alone, and my pulse races. I doubt it's because I'm excited to win the maze race. Cole takes my hand and leads me through the tall rows of corn. I can hear Maggie's fading giggles as he leads me farther into the maze.

I sneeze. Allergies. How romantic. Cole doesn't appear to notice, tugging me onto a conveniently placed haybale. I try getting comfortable, but the hay scratches even through my jeans.

"Nick ID'd the man in the picture with Robert." Cole doesn't waste any time but gets straight to the point. "His name is Anthony Avery, and he's the building inspector for Beaverhead County. We're not sure why Robert would want to hide their association. Nick is checking if Avery is the inspector on the senior center project."

"Anthony Avery," I say. "I haven't heard that name in a while."

"You know him?"

"No, but Daddy did. They worked together, and I remember Daddy mentioning his name a few times. Actually, he and Mamma were discussing Anthony Avery a few days before they died. I think it was something about a project Mr. Avery was working on, and Daddy sounded mad."

Cole's eyebrows go up. "I'd forgotten your dad was also a building inspector."

I nod. "That's one reason Sly made the Emerson Senior Center her class project. Daddy had been looking forward to being the inspector for the site. I guess they assigned Anthony Avery after ..." My voice trails off.

Cole takes my hand. "Can you recall any more details of your parents' conversation?" he asks.

I close my eyes, remembering. "They were sitting at the kitchen table, drinking coffee. Mamma had made Daddy's favorite molasses cookies." I can practically smell the fragrance of the cookies, transported back in time. "There'd been a watermain break at the junior high school that day, so the principal dismissed us early."

"Yeah, I remember that day. The high school kids were mad because our water worked fine. We had to stay in class while you all left early."

I sink deeper into the memory. "I heard Daddy's voice when I walked in the door. He sounded angry, which surprised me. I guess I crept towards the kitchen because they didn't realize I was standing there for several minutes. Daddy said something like Mr. Avery was dishonest. I didn't understand what they were talking about, so there wasn't much context for me.

"I remember Mamma sounded worried," I whisper, scooting closer to Cole. "She squeezed Daddy's hand and said, 'I trust you'll do the right thing.' But I got the feeling she wished he wouldn't. It was weird."

I look up at Cole, who studies me closely. For a minute, I forget what we were discussing while we simply look at each other. The sound of Maggie's laughter interrupts the stare-off, and we both glance away.

Cole clears his voice. "Well, that raises some questions about the integrity of Anthony Avery. If your dad mistrusted him, then it's worth investigating his connection with Robert. I'll tell Nick what you remember, and he can take it from there."

I nod and start to stand, but Cole takes my hand and pulls me down beside him.

"Jess, let Nick do the investigating from now on, okay? When I think of what might have happened last night ..." He trails off.

I'm not sure how to read his expression. Worry. Concern. Care. My pulse flips a little, but I can't look away.

"I'm sorry," is all I can say.

It must be the right response because Cole leans closer. I have the frantic thought *He's going to kiss me. Where are my tic-tacs?* Suddenly, Maggie's voice sounds a lot nearer than we expect. Or want, to be honest.

Cole pulls back with a small grin. "To be continued." He stands, pulling me with him. "Hey, Magpie, over here," Cole calls out.

A second later, Maggie and Grace round the corner and face us.

"I thought we were racing," Grace says with a knowing smile. "Do you concede?"

"Happily." I'm eager to leave the maze, so I can be alone to think.

I have a lot on my mind.

16

Wednesday, September 19
6:30 p.m.

It's the perfect night for a bonfire. Our church owns several acres of land, where we have picnics, youth group gatherings, and sometimes an old-fashioned camp meeting. One of my favorite events is our annual all-church retreat. The entire congregation spends the weekend camping in tents and RVs.

The leaves have been falling for several weeks now, and the grass is barely visible under the colorful blanket of red and gold. The BoB group will rake the leaves, clean up the grounds, and then it will be s'mores time. I can't wait to burn some marshmallows. Grace picks out our section and waves me over to join her.

"Well, this is fun." I send leaves flying with my rake.

"These leaves just fell in the last couple of days," she points out. "Wait until we dig down to the soggy ones molded to the ground. That'll be a workout." She pokes at a particularly stubborn area of grass. "Anything new with Sly?"

For a minute, I'm startled, thinking she's asking about Sly and Nick. Then I realize she wants to hear what's happening with the arrest. It's tempting to describe the interactions Cole and I witnessed between Sly and Nick. But I haven't discussed it with Sly yet, and it doesn't feel like something I can share—even with Grace.

"Nick says they're continuing to investigate this Anthony Avery guy. They asked the prosecutors to wait on Sly's case until they can find more facts. In a way, this is good news for Sly, but she just wants it done." I pat my leaf pile with the flat of my rake, so the wind won't send them flying.

"My mom told me she saw Sly at the library yesterday."

"Yep, she had an interview," I explain. "She said it sounds like a job she'd enjoy, but it doesn't pay a lot. She may have to work two part-time jobs."

Grace notices my tone and drops her rake to come and stand near me. "Jess, I know this is hard for you and your sisters, especially after everything else you've lost. But remember, you all have people who love you. Our family prays for you every time we have devotions together. God *will* take care of you. Can you believe that?"

I'm touched by her solemn words. It's not that Grace doesn't have a relationship with God—she does. But mostly, she's kind of private and less vocal about what she believes.

"Hey, slackers," Kellen's voice echoes across the field.

We laugh and wave, and Grace bends to pick up her rake.

"Um, guess what?" Grace focuses on a section of matted leaves.

"You know I'm a terrible guesser," I grumble. "Tell me."

She gives a small smile. "Kellen asked me to Homecoming."

"He did what?" I exclaim.

She peers around, obviously not wanting to draw attention. "Shh, not so loud."

"But wait, I'm confused. Kellen doesn't attend our high school. He's homeschooled."

"Yes. But if I sign a request, I can invite anyone, even if they aren't part of our school."

"Huh." I start to rake again. "But how did he know about our Homecoming?"

"I told him," she says. "On our date Monday afternoon."

My jaw drops. "Your date? You went on a date with Kellen and didn't even tell me?" My voice gets louder with each word.

She shushes me again. "Well, it wasn't actually a planned date," she clarifies. "After I left the Pumpkin Patch, I went home, showered, and went downtown for an eggnog milkshake."

I shudder.

Grace grins. "See, I remembered how much you hate those, so I spared you the trauma. I was standing in line, and Kellen joined me. When I ordered my shake, he asked the server to put it on his bill."

I raise an eyebrow. "Okay." I roll my hand to say, 'go on.'

"Kellen said he wanted to pay for my shake, so he could count it as our first date. That way, he could skip all the first date nerves." Grace beams like she thinks Kellen is a genius.

He kind of is.

"Anyway," she resumes, "we drank our shakes and talked for over an hour. When I mentioned you and Cole going to Homecoming together, Kellen asked who I was going with. I said no one, and he asked if he could take me."

She's focusing on the edges of the leaf pile, acting nonchalant. But I know my friend—she's excited to attend Homecoming with Kellen.

"Great. Maybe we can go to dinner together. I'll check with Cole if you want."

She seems relieved. "I hoped you'd say that. I want to spend time with Kellen, but I'm just getting to know him. It would be a lot more fun to go with you and Cole."

I give Grace an awkward hug around my rake. "Of course, I don't mind. Let's talk to the guys during the bonfire." I wave at the crew filling enormous bags with everyone's leaves. "Over here," I call. "We're ready for bagging."

Grace and I place our rakes in the back of Pastor Jarrod's

pickup. Then, we wander over to the bonfire and watch Anna lay out hot dogs, buns, and s'mores ingredients on a camp table.

"Can we help?" I sneak a marshmallow from the bag.

"Sure," Anna says. "Will you grab the mustard and ketchup from the Walmart sack in my car?"

As Grace hurries off to retrieve the items, I scan the area. I spot Macy sitting on a log, staring at the fire.

"Be right back," I say.

Anna glances over at Macy, then nods. "Good idea."

I stroll to where Macy sits and plop down beside her.

"Hi," I say, realizing I have no idea what else to say. I haven't talked to Macy since she shared her story. "How's it going?"

Macy jumps. Deep in her thoughts, she didn't even realize I'm sitting beside her.

"Oh, hi, Jess." She gives me a genuine smile. "I'm fine. How are you?"

"I'm ready for s'mores." Relieved, I try to keep it light.

"Well, I'm fixated on the hot dogs," she says. "I'm allergic to chocolate, so no s'mores for me."

My mouth falls open. "Allergic to chocolate?" I stare in disbelief. "Like, forever?"

She nods. "I mean, I can eat it and not die or anything, but it makes me super sick, so I just don't."

"You should get in the prayer line for that," I blurt out.

"Maybe." She laughs. "I guess I never think of asking God to heal me. He has more important things to worry about than whether or not I can eat a Snickers bar."

I shrug. "He might surprise you. My mamma used to quote a scripture that says, 'you have not because you ask not.' It doesn't hurt to ask."

"Your mom sounds like a smart lady." Macy smiles. "Please introduce us next Sunday."

My own smile falters, and I look away. "Um, Mamma and Daddy died last year in a car accident."

She gasps and puts her hand on my arm, "Oh, Jess, I'm so

sorry. I've focused on my own stuff, and I haven't asked Todd and Terri about the other people in the group." Her eyes mist with tears.

"Hey, it's okay. You didn't know. I don't discuss it much these days, now that we're dealing with my sister's problems."

She looks confused, so I tell her about Sly's arrest.

"Have you ever wondered how we'd face all these problems if we couldn't pray or trust God?" Macy asks. "How do people cope when they don't have Jesus in their lives?"

"I never thought of it that way before," I admit. "I mean, this is all I've ever known. First, I watched my parent's faith, and then almost two years ago, I made my own decision to be a Christ-follower. Not everyone believes the way we do, but I never considered how they handle difficult things in their lives."

I have a sudden picture of Amy Sinclair, the day she made those accusations against Sly. My face flushes as I visualize her in the dirt, screaming, 'Get her out of here!' I doubt Amy is a believer, and I certainly haven't given her any reason to think Christians are very loving and forgiving. I need to apologize.

"Let's eat," Pastor Jarrod shouts.

In moments, BoB members surround us, grabbing roasting sticks and jostling for a place near the fire. Macy and I smile at each other, silently promising to continue our conversation later.

I like Macy, and although I'm sorry for what she went through in Tennessee, I'm glad she's here with us now.

Cole jogs to where I sit and pulls me to my feet. "All good?"

"All good," I assure him. And it is.

Wednesday, September 19
9:00 p.m.

COLE TAKES ME HOME, and we're surprised to see Nick's squad car parked in my driveway when we arrive.

Sly and Nick sit at the kitchen table, eating brownies and ice cream.

She nods toward the counter where the brownie pan sits. "Help yourself."

I get plates for Cole and me.

"I'm giving Sly an update." Nick says, "Anthony Avery is the inspector assigned to the Emerson Senior Homes project Sinclair Construction is building."

"So, he had a legitimate reason to visit Robert at the site," Cole says. "Why the secrecy? Assuming those pictures are why Robert took the camera."

"Sly's pictures show evidence of substandard lumber," Nick says. "The lumber is clearly marked 'utility-grade,' although the specs for that type of project require No.1 lumber. I'm sure Robert doesn't want anyone to see those photos."

"If Sinclair Construction used that utility grade lumber, it would compromise the strength of the building. In fact, it could be unsafe and might cost thousands of dollars in damages. In the worst case, it could even cause deaths if the building collapsed."

"But why would Robert take that chance?" I ask.

Cole raises the carton of ice cream he retrieved from the freezer. I nod, and he scoops some on our brownies.

"Money," Nick answers my question. "It's possible he charged the Emerson company for No 1-grade lumber, purchased the much cheaper utility grade, and pocketed the difference. That's usually how those scams work."

While Cole returns the ice cream to the freezer, I grab our plates and carry them to the table, joining Nick and Sly. First s'mores, then brownies and ice cream. I hope my dress still fits me by Saturday.

Nick glances at Sly. "Aren't you all wondering how I know so much about lumber grades?"

She grins and flutters her eyelashes. "I assumed you know everything about everything."

Cole snorts and chokes on his brownie. I pat him on the back.

Nick ignores his brother and turns to Sly. "Well, I had a crash course in building codes today. Compliments of the FBI."

"The FBI?" I sputter. "How did they get involved in this?"

"When I started making inquiries concerning Anthony Avery, an alert was sent to the FBI field office in Missoula. I received a phone call from Special Agent Jack Dunn, who asked why I was interested in Mr. Avery. We compared notes, and I was told they suspect Avery of taking bribes from construction companies and private individuals. They pay him to overlook any faulty or substandard materials they might use in their construction projects."

Nick reaches down to touch Sly's hand. "Special Agent Dunn was very happy to get the SD card with your pictures. He said this is the first actual evidence they have. It should be enough for a warrant to investigate Avery's other projects, too."

"The FBI has my pictures?" Sly eyes widen. "Is this for real?"

"It's as real as it gets," Nick confirms. "They plan to execute the search tomorrow, starting at the Emerson site. If they used utility-grade lumber in the framing, the FBI will arrest Anthony Avery and Robert Sinclair for fraud."

"That's great," I say. "But what about the charges against Sly?"

"I'm sure that will be part of the conversation the District Attorney will have with Robert," Nick explains. "Sheriff Richards and I hope we can drop all charges against her soon."

Tears burn my eyes, and when Cole reaches to take my hand, I lightly squeeze his. Sly and Nick are having a similar moment as he draws my weeping sister into his arms.

Cole tugs me up and whispers, "Let's move to the porch."

I follow him outside and drop onto the swing. I'm pleased when he sits close to me, wrapping his arm around my shoulders. He pushes against the porch floor, and the swing glides gently back and forth. We sit in silence for a few minutes, absorbing the news Nick shared.

"I'm scared to believe it," I finally say. "What if something goes wrong, and they can't prove Robert lied about Sly? What if she still goes to jail?" I shiver a little from the cool night air, but also from fear. "What if we are close, but it isn't enough?"

"I have an idea," Cole whispers.

My mind is racing, and I barely register his words. I need a plan.

"Jess," Cole says.

"Now that I know about the building fraud," I interrupt him, "I could go back to Robert's office and try to find more evidence."

He tenses and turns to look at me.

"Jessica."

Cole rarely calls me Jessica. He's serious.

"The FBI will search for evidence. You won't."

I start to protest.

Cole shakes his head. "You. Won't."

"Fine," I say, a little miffed. Under my breath, I mutter, "Bossy, much?"

I'm pretty sure he hears, but he ignores me.

"I have an idea," he repeats.

I perk up. "What?"

"Prayer," Cole says.

I snort. "What do you think I've been doing?" I demand.

He studies me. "You've been praying?"

I don't appreciate the incredulous tone of his voice. "Of course."

"Great." He nods. "Now, why don't we try the Matthew 18:19 kind of prayer?"

"Um, I'm not sure what kind that is," I confess. There are different types of prayers? Who knew?

Cole answers, "In Matthew 18:19, Jesus said, 'if two of you agree on earth about anything they may ask, it will be done for them by My Father in heaven.' We could pray together and ask God to send justice for Sly."

"Yes," I say, "I think that's a perfect idea."

In the quiet of the September evening, Cole and I pray for justice.

17

Friday, September 21
3:30 p.m.

"All right, ladies, buckle up." Grace's older brother, Matt, pulls his Camry away from the curb, honking and waving at the students walking near the high school.

Matt is 19 and attends Mountainview Community College, where he's studying to be a phlebotomist, which is a fancy word for people who draw blood. The other day he asked if he could practice on Grace and me, but we politely refused. Well, if you can call screaming, 'Get away from us, you monster,' being polite.

Today, there are no needles in sight. We're relaxed as Matt drives us to Dillon for a quick shopping trip. Tomorrow night is the Homecoming dance, and although we have our dresses, Grace says we need to accessorize, whatever that means.

Usually, if the rubber band in my hair doesn't clash with my outfit, I call it good. But I concede since this is Homecoming, I should up my game. Grace wants to visit an antique store in Dillon call Verity's, where she likes to buy vintage jewelry. I have my earrings and necklace, but I still haven't found a clutch, and I doubt my bookbag will pass Sly's inspection. Or Grace's.

Matt drops us at Verity's, telling us to 'make it quick,' since he has a date tonight. Matt plans to pick up his re-soled boots. Unless Mr. Murphy keeps Matt talking, we figure we have twenty minutes for shopping.

As we enter the shop, a small bell tinkles, announcing our arrival. Verity herself sits on a stool behind the counter. She's one of those women who might be any age from 50 to 70. She wears a plain denim dress, but somehow, she makes it look classy. Her silver hair is fastened in a messy bun, and several turquoise bracelets jangle as she hurries over to greet us.

"Grace," she exclaims. "Oh, sweetie, I haven't seen you in ages. And you've brought a friend, too. Please come in and sit awhile. I can get us some tea." Verity moves to a small table that holds a teapot, cups, and a few cookies.

My nose tells me they are freshly baked oatmeal raisin, one of my favorites. I walk toward the table, remembering my skipped lunch. I'd finished my homework instead of eating, so my weekend would be free.

Grace grabs my arm, pulling me away from the snacks. "I'm happy to see you too, Verity. And I wish we could visit, but I'm afraid we need to hurry, or Matt might leave us to walk home."

I eye the cookies with longing as Grace tugs me toward the boutique area that displays the purses and jewelry.

"I understand," Verity says, with genuine disappointment. "But let's make the most of the time you do have. What are you looking for today?" Verity walks over and hands each of us a napkin holding two cookies.

They're still warm. I turn to express my undying gratitude.

Verity smiles, winks, and pats my hand. "I was a schoolgirl once, too, you know."

I savor the cookies while Grace chats with Verity about what type of accessories she wants. Wandering over to a table, I notice a black velvet pouch purse with three small roses embroidered near the bottom. The bag closes with a drawstring that I judge is long enough to dangle from my wrist. I check the price tag and blink. Oh, well, I don't need a purse. My dress has pockets.

I turn aside, watching Grace hold up a pair of dangling pearl earrings to the light. They are delicate, not too long, and perfect for her. I walk around the store and finish my cookies, and one of Grace's, while Verity wraps the earrings in tissue paper and takes the payment.

"Did you find a purse?" Grace accepts the earring bag from Verity.

"I think I'll do fine with the pockets in my dress." I steal one last look over at the black velvet purse. It's gone. I turn around, surprised to see Grace and Verity smiling at me.

Verity holds out another tissue-wrapped package. "I'll put this in a sack for you."

"Oh, no," I protest.

"Jess." Verity wraps my fingers around the paper bag holding the velvet purse.

The sadness in her voice surprises me.

"You don't remember me, I'm sure. How could you, when the only time you saw me was at your parents' funeral. You see, I was your mother's friend. She often stopped in here to look, and sometimes even buy a special treasure.

We spent many Saturday afternoons sipping tea and talking. She loved you girls so much ..." Verity's voice breaks, and she glances away, then turns back and says briskly, "There now, I didn't mean to make you sad, my dear."

I wipe at my tears. "Maybe I could come over some Saturday, and we could talk about my mamma?"

Verity gives me a light hug, "Please do."

I open my wallet.

"And Jess," she stills my hands, "let me gift this purse to you, sweetheart. In honor of your sweet Mamma and my dear friend."

I nod, unable to speak for a moment. "Thank you," I whisper.

Verity gives a satisfied nod, hugs Grace, and ushers us to the door as Matt pulls up.

"Have fun, my dears," she calls, waving as we ride away.

Friday, September 21
8:30 p.m.

I SCRUNCH down in the seat of the double recliner, pulling the popcorn bowl onto my lap.

"Hey," Grace protests from her seat at the other end.

I grab a handful of popcorn and place the bowl between us. "Relax. This is all I want. I'm still full from dinner. Sly made meatloaf."

Grace looks hurt. "And you didn't smuggle me any? You know how much I love Sly's meatloaf."

I nod. "This is true. That girl can cook. We have plenty left if you want to stop over when we're done here."

Here is the Ellison's family room. Grace has been with the twins since we returned from Dillon. We planned to attend the football game tonight, but when Mrs. Ellison called in a panic, Grace didn't have the heart to say no. And I didn't have the heart to make Grace spend the evening alone.

Mr. Ellison was traveling home from a business meeting in Bozeman when his car broke down. It was towed to a service station, but Mrs. Ellison needed to pick him up. Since Bozeman is over two hours each way from Justice, we don't expect them back until 11:00 p.m.

The twins went to bed at 8:00, and we experienced a genuine miracle—they actually went to sleep. Now we're relaxing while attempting to keep each other awake. It's been an exhausting week already, and tomorrow is packed.

We crunch our popcorn in silence for a few minutes.

"Jess, can I ask you a question?" Grace says.

Grace and I have been best friends since the day she arrived in Justice nine months earlier. I guess that doesn't sound like a long time, but I figure it's the quality, not the quantity that counts. I met Grace three weeks after my parents' funeral when her family moved to town and started attending my church. We made an immediate connection that has only deepened.

Consequently, I'm familiar with Grace's tones. This particular question, in this particular tone, worries me. She wants to have a serious conversation.

I try joking. "You did ask me a question."

Not even a glimpse of a smile. Okay then, serious it is.

"Yes." I lean back, closing my eyes in the hope Grace might take pity on me and let me sleep.

She's pitiless. "Why do you blame yourself for your parents' deaths?"

My eyes fly open, and I sit up, nearly dumping the popcorn. "Wow, Gracie, way to blindside me." Sometimes offense is the best defense.

She reaches over the popcorn bowl to touch my arm. "I didn't say it to hurt you, but I'm pretty sure you knew what I was going to ask, anyway."

I shrug and face her, settling into the recliner again. It looks like we're going to have this conversation.

"It *is* my fault," I mutter.

Grace doesn't seem shocked by my words or even surprised. "Did you make their car go off the road and into that ravine?"

Tears sting my eyes as I shake my head, "No, but ..."

"But nothing. I don't understand why you've been blaming yourself all this time. My mom calls it survivor's guilt, but I think there's more to it, right?"

"Why are you doing this?" I practically wail the words.

"Because you're my friend, and I love you."

I lose the war with my tears, and now they roll down my

cheeks in what feels like rivers. "It's my fault they were on that road. I wanted a guitar for my birthday. And not just any kind, either. A man in Bozeman was selling an Ovation guitar, and I convinced Daddy and Mamma I wanted it for my Christmas gift.

Sly told me later they decided not to wait but surprise me on my birthday, instead. They were on their way to buy the guitar when the accident happened."

Grace moves the popcorn to the floor and scoots over to hug me. "Oh, Jess, I'm so sorry. I had no idea. What a terrible weight to carry all this time, especially when you didn't have to."

I use the sleeve of my sweatshirt to swipe at my face. "It's my fault," I repeat.

"Your dad was driving that afternoon. Is it his fault they died?"

I jerk away from her. "Of course not! It was an accident."

"Exactly." She watches me as I absorb her statement. "How do you think your parents would feel if they knew you've been blaming yourself for what happened? Is that what they would want for you?"

I shake my head, my throat tightening.

"You weren't responsible for what happened then," Grace continues, "and you aren't responsible for what's happening now."

I look up, surprised.

"You're such a loving, loyal sister. But it's not your responsibility to fix things for your family. In fact, recent events show that may lead to more trouble." She raises one eyebrow.

"D'ya think?" I give a reluctant smile.

"I think," she agrees. "Can I ask another question?"

"Might as well, since I'm already a blubbering mess."

"This is the very first time I've ever heard you mention playing the guitar. Why don't you play anymore?"

I shrug, "I guess I don't have the heart. I still have the old Fender that Daddy used for my lessons, but it hasn't even been out of the case since the accident. Somehow, I didn't think I deserve to play anymore."

Grace's blue eyes swim with tears. "Your dad taught you how to play?"

I nod.

"Jess, that is such a gift he gave you. Obviously, your music was on their minds and hearts. Please don't let that be taken from you, too."

I reach over to squeeze her hand. Then we sit in silence for a minute.

"Grace, can I ask you a question?"

She gives a tentative nod.

"How'd you get to be so smart?"

18

Saturday, September 22
10:30 a.m.

"Hurry up, Jess. The DMV closes at noon on Saturday, and it's already 10:30." Sly's voice echoes up the stairway.

I picture her standing near the railing, tapping her foot impatiently. Sly is a tapper.

"Coming," I holler down the hallway as I turn off my computer and grab my bag. I've spent the last several hours taking practice tests online, preparing for today's exciting event. Or at least this is the first exciting event of the day. Tonight is the Homecoming dance. I guess I prefer to cram all my stress into one twelve-hour time period.

I'm using Sly's Honda for the test. Sliding into the driver's seat, I grab the keys from her and reach for the ignition.

She puts her hand over mine. "Wait."

I raise an eyebrow. "I thought you said we're in a hurry."

"We are," she agrees, "but you need to take a deep breath and relax. You've got this. Besides, we should pray before we go."

My other eyebrow lifts. "You said I've got this."

"You do." She reaches down to pull her seatbelt around and

buckle it. Tight. Then she grasps my hand and prays, "Father, please give Jess the confidence she needs to pass this test today. Help her remember everything she's learned and give her favor with the instructor."

We both say, "Amen."

Then I'm pulling out of the driveway, headed for the DMV office in downtown Justice.

It's a relief that there's only one person in line ahead of me when we arrive. I heard that Tyler Conklin is making his second attempt at passing the driver's portion of the test. Two weeks ago, he'd pulled his car up to the DMV building and promptly drove over the instructor's big toe. Tyler protested when he automatically failed, claiming the test hadn't officially started since Mr. Davidson wasn't in the car yet.

Now, I stand behind Tyler, who gives me a cocky grin.

"Look out, everybody," he calls. "Jess Thomas will be loose on the road."

I want to point out he's the one who broke Mr. Davidson's toe, but I keep my mouth shut.

A clerk whose name tag reads *Elaine* peers up from her computer. "Tyler, Sheriff Richards will give you the driving test today. He's headed over from the jail, so have a seat." She motions for Tyler to step back and let me approach the counter.

Tyler turns a little pale, and I kind of feel sorry for him. Sheriff Richards worked for the DMV before his election, and he still helps out occasionally. It's rumored he gets the tough cases. Yep, Tyler definitely qualifies. I'm grateful I won't be riding with the Sheriff.

Elaine hands me the questions, and I sit on an uncomfortable plastic orange chair, whisper a prayer, and write.

Fifteen minutes later, I return the booklet to Elaine. She checks the test, tells me I missed one question, then says to have a seat. I turn to give Sly a thumbs-up.

Tyler is still waiting for Sheriff Richards to arrive. I step around him and sit next to Sly.

"Good job," she whispers.

I don't get why people think they have to whisper at the DMV. It's not the library. I'm whispering that observation to Sly when a side door opens, and Mr. Davidson limps in. He makes a wide circle around Tyler, then heads to the counter. He takes some papers from Elaine, glances at them and then me.

"Jessica Thomas?" he asks, looking at me over his wire-rim glasses.

"Yes, sir." I step toward him and hold out my hand. "How are you today, sir?"

"Just peachy," Mr. Davidson says, clearly not. He glances at my hand with a puzzled frown, and then he gives it a quick shake.

Great. I've probably broken some DMV rule about not touching the instructor.

"Let's go." He shuffles to the front door.

I follow, giving Sly a wave as I leave. "It's a beautiful day, isn't it?" I lead him to Sly's car. "I'm glad it's not raining. That would make it even harder for me to take the test." I do what I always do when I'm nervous—I talk. Very fast. "Not that the test will be too hard. Or too easy. I'm sure you'll make it as difficult as you can." I wince.

His mouth twitches a little.

I feel fairly confident at first. I've been driving on my learner's permit for over a year now, so I have lots of practice. But I know that eventually, we'll reach the part I've been dreading— parallel parking. I consider asking if there's a form I can sign promising to never, ever parallel park so I can skip that part.

After driving for twenty minutes, we head toward the DMV building. I hope he's forgotten parallel parking. Maybe he's anxious to get back because he has to go to the bathroom. I know I do.

We're less than a block from the entrance to the parking lot when Mr. Davidson instructs, "slow down and parallel park between those two cars." He nods toward a small VW and Sheriff Richards' squad car.

I gape at him in panic. "There?" I squeak.

"There," he confirms.

I nibble my lower lip as I pull next to the squad car. Turning the steering wheel, I angle Sly's Honda toward the curb and start backing slowly into the space between the two vehicles. After I move past the squad car, I turn the wheel again and carefully straighten the car into the parking space. I give him a triumphant look.

"Ms. Thomas?" Mr. Davidson scribbles something down in his notebook. "How close is your car supposed to be to the curb when you park?"

My mind goes blank. Random numbers jump around in my brain, yelling, 'pick me, pick me.' "Um, an, uh, adequate amount?" I answer.

He glances up, obviously deciding if I'm serious or being a smart aleck. "Hmmm," is all he says.

I hope I can leave Sly's Honda where it is and we can walk the block to the office. Sly can have the pleasure of pulling her car out of the tight spot between the VW and the Sheriff's car.

Mr. Davidson points toward the DMV building. "Take us home, Ms. Thomas."

But no such luck.

Ten minutes and one exceptionally horrific license photo later, Sly and I are on our way home.

Saturday, September 22
12:15 p.m.

THE REST of the afternoon passes in a strange, too slow/too fast pace. We arrive home as Maggie is leaving on her bike to go visit her friend, Rachel.

"Be back by 5:00 if you want to see Jess before she leaves," Sly calls as we race up the front steps.

Maggie waves over her shoulder and pedals away.

Sly hurries into the kitchen and rattles around in the fridge. "Left-over meatloaf or ..." she sniffs an open Tupperware container. "Tuna salad." The way she mutters, "tuna salad" makes it sound as if she can't be entirely sure of the contents.

"I'm not very hungry."

Sly shakes her head. "You're nervous and excited, but the last thing you need is to pass out from lack of food."

I figure I'm several meals away from that happening. But she's in 'Mom' mode, so I give in and mix up some peanut butter and maple syrup like Daddy taught me. I slather it on a piece of bread, which I fold in half and take a bite.

"See, I'm eating," but it comes out, *thee, I'm teething*.

Sly laughs. "You're such a goofus." But affection fills her tone.

I grab a bottle of green tea from the fridge and twist off the lid, taking a deep swallow.

"So, what's the plan?" Sly asks, practically rubbing her hands together like an evil mastermind from a cartoon show.

"Plan?" I ask, honestly puzzled.

"The. Plan." She speaks the words separately. "Tonight is Homecoming, remember? Do you want to start with a mani/pedi, or maybe put your hair up in rollers? Did you wipe off your black heels, as I suggested? I think you stepped in some mud the last time you wore them." She grabs a banana from the fruit bowl.

"Mani/pedi?" I ask dumbly. "I mean, I know what that is, I've just never heard the words in connection with myself."

"Jess, I thought you and Grace discussed this when you two were shopping for her dress last week," Sly says, evidently striving for patience. "There's a lot more to getting ready for Homecoming than simply taking a shower and putting on a dress."

"I have to shower, too?" I exclaim. Sometimes it's so easy to tease her.

For a second, I think I've gone too far because it seems like she might scream with frustration. Then she sees my face and relaxes.

"Very funny," she says in what Maggie calls Sly's sarcasm-y voice.

"Relax. Grace will be here at 1:00 p.m. to start our transformation. I'm not sure if there will be a mani/pedi, but she is bringing tons of hair junk and makeup goo."

She still doesn't seem to know if I'm kidding or not, but she lets it go.

"Okay. You're in good hands with Grace." Sly opens the cabinet door under the sink and tosses the banana peel in the trash can.

"Um, tell me again what the schedule is for tonight?" Before I can reply, she answers her own question. "So, Kellen will drive to Cole's house, and the guys will drive here in Cole's dad's Mazda, right? Pictures at 5:00 p.m., then dinner at Alberto's in Dillon. You'll get back to town around 7:30 and attend the dance. Afterward, you're going to the bonfire at Todd and Terri's, right? And home by 12:30 a.m., sharp."

I nod all the way through the schedule recitation. "Yep." I agree. "What exciting plans do you and Maggie have this evening?" I finish my green tea.

"Actually, Maggie is spending the night at Rachel's house and meeting us at church tomorrow. After we finish the pictures, I'll run her over to Rachel's." She grabs a dishtowel and wipes at a non-existent spot on the kitchen counter.

"I feel guilty that we're leaving you on your own for the evening," I say.

"Um, well, I won't be totally alone," she responds, scrubbing harder.

Sly has a *tell*, like when people play card games, and they always do the same thing if they have good cards. When she's nervous, she cleans. The counter is gleaming.

"Hey." I walk over and take the towel from her hands. "Talk to me. What are you doing tonight?" I have a flash picture of her being hauled away by prison guards while I'm dancing the night away with Cole.

She gives a shy smile. "Well, I have a date, too. Nick and I are going to a movie in Dillon. We'll probably grab something to eat on the way back. But don't worry, I'll have plenty of time to hear all about your night."

I smile at the excitement in my sister's eyes. "I'm not the only one who will have a story to tell," I tease. "The McBride brothers and the Thomas sisters. That's kind of ..." I start to say weird.

"Interesting," Sly finishes my sentence with a soft smile. "Very interesting."

19

"Y ou're sure?" I ask Grace for the zillionth time.

"Absolutely positive," she replies with the patience of Job.

We're staring at our reflections in the full-length mirror attached to my closet door.

I smooth down the soft velvet of my skirt and give her a shaky smile. "We clean up pretty good."

"We do," Grace agrees, tucking a stray strand of hair behind my ear.

She spent forever curling my hair, and now it rests in soft waves on my shoulders. We pulled one side back and secured it with a silver barrette. I'm wearing Sly's almost-diamond stud earrings and my *J*-shaped silver necklace. It was a gift from Mamma and Daddy, and I wear it on special occasions.

My black heels, minus the mud, are perfect with the dress. They are strappy but easy to walk in. I keep staring at the mirror, unable to believe my eyes.

Grace stands beside me, looking like a Disney princess. She

wears a sapphire blue skater dress with a lace overlay. Her strawberry blonde hair is in an up-do with wispy dangling curls around her face. She's wearing the pearl earrings she purchased from Verity and a thin silver necklace with three small pearls in the center. She's stunning.

The doorbell rings, and Grace and I stare into the mirror with a mixture of panic and excitement.

"Showtime," she whispers.

"You go first." I give Grace a gentle push toward the door. "That way, you can break my fall if I trip down the steps."

I hear voices in the foyer, then a sudden silence as Grace walks down the stairs. I smile, picturing Kellen's jaw dropping when he sees her.

"Okay, Jess, your turn," Sly calls.

Taking a deep breath, I step to the landing. I fight a persistent picture of me tumbling down to land at Cole's feet in a Homecoming heap. Not going to happen. Focusing on my feet, I reach the bottom of the steps then glance up to see Cole staring. At me. I can't decipher his expression since it's one I've never, ever seen before.

"Jess," Cole says. He seems to be out of words, so he repeats that one again. "Jess."

"Cole," I respond teasingly.

He isn't smiling, and I get nervous. What if he came to tell me he invited someone else to Homecoming, and this is all a terrible misunderstanding?

"You're beautiful."

If I hadn't seen his lips move, I wouldn't have thought it was Cole talking because his voice is husky and a little breathless.

I want to say, "You, too," because he is. Beautiful, that is.

Cole's wearing a black suit, white shirt, and a thin tie matching his gray eyes. He looks terrific and smells amazing. I feel breathless myself.

He holds a white florist box and opens it to show me a wrist corsage nestled inside. The tiny pink and crimson roses will be perfect with my dress and velvet bag.

Kellen is also wearing a black suit, and his shirt is the same shade of blue as Grace's dress. He helps Grace with her corsage, and then we step out onto the porch so Sly can take pictures. Maggie rides up on her bike and oohs and aahs over us.

We climb into Cole's dad's car. I sit beside Cole as he drives, and Kellen and Grace ride in the back. For the first several minutes, we're quiet, each taking quick glances at our dates and then looking out the window. It's like when there's an eclipse, and you can't look directly at the sun.

The restaurant is fifteen minutes away. By the time we arrive, the awkwardness has disappeared, and we're returning to normal-ish. Cole parks the car, and as he gets out, I reach for the door handle.

"Jess," Grace hisses from the back seat, "Wait."

When Cole helps me out of the car, I realize my mistake. We walk to the restaurant, and Kellen opens the door so Grace and I can step through. Manners are exhausting. I make a note to watch Grace and do whatever she does tonight.

We planned to meet Todd and Hannah and Terri and her date, Caleb. I'm hungry, and the Italian food tastes delicious. But I'm also nervous, and I push my food around on my plate, so it looks like I'm eating. I notice Grace, Terri, and Hannah are all doing the same thing. The guys, however, appear unaffected by nerves, so they eat all their food, plus most of ours.

A little over an hour later, we enter the high school gymnasium. The decoration committee has transformed it with hundreds of twinkle lights and silver and blue balloons. Shimmery tulle gracefully loops over the rafters of the gym ceiling. It even smells good, which is a miracle. This gym has seen a lot of tears, sweat, and worse. The committee did an outstanding job.

The event started a half-hour earlier, and many couples are dancing. Others stand along the wall like they're ready to play a dressed-up version of dodge ball. Heart pounding, I realize this is the moment of truth. I have to dance with Cole. Correction, I *get* to dance with Cole.

"Are you okay?" Cole glances down at me.

I can tell he knows what I'm thinking.

"We don't have to dance, Jess, if you don't want to."

"No," I say. "I mean, yes, I do want to dance. But can we start over there in the corner?" I point to a shadowed area that has few twinkle lights. "Just until we get the hang of it?"

"Good idea." Cole takes my hand, and we walk toward the small alcove. I watch Kellen lead Grace onto the actual dance floor, which is okay because she can actually dance.

We stop, and Cole raises my hand and lays it on his shoulder. His hand rests lightly on my waist, and he sways us back and forth.

"Relax," he leans down and whispers in my ear. "You're doing great."

And I *am* doing great. All the intimidation leaves, and I relax, enjoying the experience. After a few minutes, Cole slow dances us onto the dance floor, and we join the party. For the next hour, I dance with Cole, Kellen, Todd, and then Cole again. This is fun!

Until it isn't. Mark Crowley and Amy Sinclair bump-dance into us, and I lose my balance.

Cole steadies me and gives Mark a sharp look. "Careful there," is all Cole says, though.

My heart pounds. Why is Mark even at the dance tonight? I thought he was still recovering from his injuries. He seems to be moving a little slowly, and I notice he still wears a cast on his left arm. I wonder if the bump was truly an accident. Either way, I don't want Mark and Cole anywhere near each other.

I still haven't told Cole that Mark took me to Bannack. Common sense would say that Mark will keep his mouth shut, too, but who knows? Common sense and Mark Crowley don't seem to be on speaking terms.

Amy snickers. "Oops, so sorry," she says.

I think I'll postpone apologizing for attacking her at Hadley's. Mark steps closer to Cole and seems ready to speak when Kellen and Grace appear beside us.

"Hey, Cole," Kellen says. "I think we should head to Todd and Terri's for the bonfire now."

Cole looks at Mark, who is scowling at Kellen.

"Sure," Cole says. "I think we're finished here."

A long look passes between Mark and Cole before Mark looks away and steps back.

"Hey, can you guys get the car and pick us up in a minute?" Grace suggests as we stroll through the hallway. "Jess and I want to stop in the restroom."

"We do?" I ask in surprise.

Grace gives me a look.

"Oh, yeah, that's a good idea," I say.

The guys nod and keep walking while Grace whisks me into the girl's restroom.

She glances under the stalls to make sure no one else is present. "What did Mark say to Cole?"

"Nothing, thank goodness," I say with relief. "Luckily, you and Kellen arrived at the right time."

Studying herself in the mirror, Grace smooths her hair. "Luck had nothing to do with it. I noticed Mark and Amy stalker-dancing toward you and Cole, so I suggested to Kellen that maybe we should leave." She takes out her lipstick and fills in the faded spaces, then smacks her lips and replaces the lid. "Honestly, Jess, you should tell Cole what Mark did. You don't want it to get to him through gossip."

I nibble my lower lip, and Grace frowns, handing me her lipstick.

"I don't think Mark would tell anyone he kidnapped me."

She shakes her head. "Mark believes he's above the law. I'm sure he plans to tell Cole sometime, just to dig at him. Of course, he'll pick a public place because he's too much of a coward to tell Cole in private."

I stare at her. Unfortunately, I still have Grace's lipstick against my mouth, and I draw a dark rose stripe above my upper lip.

Grace sighs and searches in her bag for a tissue, which she uses to rub away the smear.

"I'm sure Cole will be mad at Mark, but it's not like he will *do* anything to him," I mutter.

She shrugs and drops the covered lipstick back into her bag. "He might surprise you."

I nibble my lip again.

"Stop that," Grace orders as we walk out of the restroom.

Saturday, September 22
9:30 p.m.

TODD AND TERRI'S dad has the bonfire blazing when we arrive. Macy's mom flew in from Nashville this afternoon, and they join the party. We scatter to change into jeans and hoodies, carefully stowing our dresses, suits, and shoes in the car. Finally, we get down to the business of burning marshmallows.

Cole walks toward me, holding three charcoal covered marshmallows on a stick.

"Mm, just the way I like them." I pull the goo from the stick and pop it into my mouth. "You have to eat it all in one bite," I explain, licking marshmallow remains from my fingers. "Otherwise, the outside will crumble, and you'll miss the best part."

"I'll take your word for it." Cole leads me to a log near the clearing. Then he pops an unroasted marshmallow into his mouth. "What?" He asks when he sees my shocked face.

"You ate it raw," I say in mock horror.

Cole laughs and gently wipes off some marshmallow from my upper lip. He stares at my lips for a long minute.

"What? Is there more?" I ask.

"Yes, there's more." Then he kisses me.

It's everything a first kiss should be. Gentle, firm, and full of promise. And a little sticky.

When Cole leans away, I open my eyes, and he smiles.

"Do you hear that?" he whispers.

"What? I don't hear anything."

"Exactly. Every time I try to kiss you, Nick and his siren drive by at precisely the wrong moment."

I look over at our friends gathered around the fire, laughing and enjoying life together. I don't know what will happen tomorrow, but right here, right now, I'm happier than I've been in a long time.

I lean my head on Cole's shoulder, the flannel of his shirt soft against my skin. "Maybe Nick did us a favor. I think this is the perfect moment."

20

Sunday, September 23
8:30 a.m.

My Tweety alarm startles me the next morning, and I'm tempted to hit snooze. Sly and I talked until 2:00 a.m., and I barely got any sleep. I slap at Tweety, and he skids off the nightstand and plops onto the floor. At least he stopped tweeting.

Forcing myself to sit up, I head for the bathroom. Since Maggie isn't here, I'll have it all to myself. My hair still has some curl left, so that will be a huge timesaver. I don't hear any noise from Sly's room or the kitchen. Maybe I should knock on her door and make sure she hasn't overslept. Sly is always up at 7:00 a.m., no matter what.

I sniff my hair, checking for smoke from the bonfire last night. There's a hint of woodsmoke, but mostly Eden Spring, and I decide it's acceptable. Maybe it can be my own signature fragrance.

Ten minutes later, I skid down the stairs wearing black jeans, black boots, and a chunky cream-colored sweater. I'm surprised to see the front door is open a little. I hurry to close it, but just as I push, Sly shoves against it from the outside. We both barely escape broken noses as the door swings back and forth.

"Hey," we say at the same time. Eloquence runs in our family.

"Why were you out there?" I ask.

Sly shimmies past me and hurries toward the kitchen. She has that, 'Give me coffee, and no one gets hurt' look in her eyes. She doesn't speak as she pours herself a cup of coffee with shaking hands.

"Sly? What's wrong? Did something happen?"

"No, something *didn't* happen," Sly says as she blows into her coffee. "That's the problem."

She hasn't even put in her Hazelnut creamer. She's definitely upset.

"Nick stopped to tell me he heard from the FBI this morning. They searched the construction site, but the lumber has disappeared. There's nothing to connect Robert Sinclair and Anthony Avery. They plan to arrest Avery based on another case, but Robert is in the clear. And I'm still accused of embezzlement." Sly's voice shakes, and her hands do too.

I reach over to gently take her coffee cup, placing it on the counter, then wrap my arms around her.

"Last night was amazing," she whispers. "I felt like I might have a future to look forward to." Sly stands and pulls a tissue from a box on the counter. "I mean, it's early, and Nick and I have only had one official date, but Jess, it seems so real, you know?" She looks at me with tears glimmering in her hazel eyes.

I nod. "I know, Sly. Cole and I noticed how you and Nick are with each other lately. It might sound corny, but it's like we can see you two falling in love right before our eyes."

Tears spill down Sly's cheeks, and she brushes them away. "Yes," she says. "That's exactly what's happening. For me, at least." She steps back and crumples the tissue in her fingers.

"Now, I could go to jail." She gives a brief laugh that doesn't sound like she thinks anything is funny. "It won't look good for Nick to have a jailbird girlfriend when he runs for Sheriff next year. Not to mention what might happen to you and Maggie. Poor Maggie. She'll never get over the nightmares." Her tears start all over again.

I shake her shoulder. "Listen to me. You are innocent. You haven't done anything wrong. It's scary, but we have to trust God. He really is our only hope. Sly, what's your favorite story from the Bible?" I ask, knowing the answer.

"David and Goliath," she says.

"Right. David and Goliath. Here is David, a kid, and he has to fight against a giant. No one expects David to survive, let alone win. 'But God,'" I repeat one of Mamma's favorite phrases.

"But God," echoes Sly. She stands up taller.

And I see when the light comes back in her eyes.

She catches my hand and pulls me toward the front door. "C'mon, let's get to church before all the good donuts disappear."

Sunday, September 23
10:30 a.m.

ALL DURING WORSHIP, I keep thinking that phrase again and again, *'But God.'* A few years earlier, Mamma and some friends from our church attended a weekend retreat in Missoula. She'd come home, rested and happy, and at our first family dinner, Daddy asked what she'd enjoyed at the conference.

"It was all so good," Mamma said, "but one particular teaching especially touched me. It was explaining how often the phrase 'but God' shows up in scripture. Repeatedly, people faced problems they thought couldn't be solved. And then there was that moment when the scripture says, 'but God,' and everything changed." Mamma smiled as she looked at each one of us. "You're going to hear me say that a lot from now on. *But God.*"

Maggie interrupts my memories when she nudges my knee.

She's standing in the aisle, prodding me to the empty seat between Sly and me. I resist her poke. I'm sitting at the end, and I like it that way. Shaking my head, I turn my legs a little so she can scoot past me. A short battle of wills follows, but I win. Maggie climbs over me, stepping on my foot as she does.

She gives me an insincere, "sorry," and settles into the chair.

A copy of the church bulletin slips from her fingers. It flutters to the floor, and I reach down to grab it. The front has a picture of a stack of pumpkins sitting under several tall stalks of sunflowers. Flipping the page, I glance at the calendar to make sure BoB is meeting this week. As I put the bulletin in my purse, I notice the scripture printed on the bottom. My heart skips a beat when I read,

> *7 He stores up wisdom for those who are honest.*
> *Like a shield, he protects the innocent.*
> *8 He makes sure that justice is done,*
> *and he protects those who are loyal to him.*
> (Proverbs 2:7-8 NCV)

Tears prick my eyes as I remember my conversation with Sly an hour earlier. I reread the verses, struck by the words 'innocent' and 'justice.' It feels like God is sending me a message that He really will help us. I carefully put the bulletin in my purse so I can show it to Sly later. The worship band plays the first chords of a song, and I stand with my sisters, trusting that God will take care of us.

Sunday, September 23
1:30 p.m.

AS A KID, I hated naps. I especially couldn't understand why my parents always took a nap on Sunday afternoons. When I got old enough to visit my friends' homes after church, I realized it wasn't only my parents. It seems like everyone older than 25 gives in to the 'Sunday Slumber,' as Daddy called it.

I'm so exhausted from my late night I barely make it through lunch. Maggie notices my sleepiness and tries to score my sweet corn muffin sitting beside my chili bowl.

"Mine," I mutter and gently smack her fingers, then prop my head in my hands. For a minute, I think fondly of the days when someone else would feed me.

My head slips off my hand, and I open my eyes as Sly grabs my bowl before I land face-first in my chili.

"Jess, go to bed." Sly clears the table. "You need a nap."

"No. I'm not tired." I realize I am tired, and I do want a nap. Nodding, I stand and stumble toward the stairs. I wonder how much of an inconvenience it would be if I nap on the steps.

Grabbing the railing, I pull myself up the steps and to my bedroom. I only run into the wall one time. Then I flop on my bed, grab my soft, green blanket, and I'm out.

The dream is short. I'm leading a Sunday School class for several young children I don't know. The kids line up, expecting me to lead them in a song. I start singing about the man who built his house upon the rock.

As I sing, Sly and Nick walk into the room and join the line. Nick is wearing his full uniform, even his hat, which is weird, since we're inside. I keep singing, and all the kids, plus Sly and Nick, act out the motions to the song.

> *The wise man built his house upon the rock,*
> *The wise man built his house upon the rock,*
> *The wise man built his house upon the rock,*
> *And the rains come tumbling down.*
> *The rains came down, and the floods came up*
> *The rains came down, and the floods came up,*
> *The rains came down, and the floods came up*
> *And the house on the rock stood firm.*

In the dream, I smile at Sly and Nick as they do the motions together, building one house instead of two. We sing the next verse:

The foolish man built his house upon the sand
The foolish man built his house upon the sand
The foolish man built his house upon the sand
And the rains came tumbling down.
The rains came down as the flood came up,
The rains came down as the floods came up,
The rains came down as the floods came up,
And the house on the sand went SPLAT!

Everyone claps their hands together to mimic the splat, and it reverberates through my brain.

I yelp myself awake, expecting the house to be falling down around me. Instead, the sky outside is dark, and rain pelts against my window. Thunder claps, and I jump, realizing that's what woke me. I lie back down and slow my breathing.

Something concerning the dream bothers me, but I can't identify what. I smile, remembering Sly and Nick acted out the song by building their house together. Then I get goosebumps. Maybe my subconscious is processing what Sly told me about wanting a future with Nick. I like that part of the dream. But I wish I could figure out why I feel so uneasy.

Sunday, September 23
7:00 p.m.

"STUPID DREAM," I say, rubbing my right elbow, which I've cracked on a steel beam. Construction sites are dangerous in the daylight, but now it's pitch black here at the Emerson Senior Center, and not even my trusty phone flashlight helps the situation. I stumble over a bucket, muttering, "C'mon guys. A clean site is a safe site."

That I'm trespassing isn't lost on me, but I decide that ship has sailed, as Daddy used to say. Daddy had a lot of fascinating sayings. I should write them down sometime.

The truth is, I have no idea what I'm looking for. Story of my life lately. The dream stayed with me all afternoon, making me restless and edgy. I hadn't planned a stop at the construction site when I left the house an hour ago. Sly had reluctantly given me the keys to her Honda for my first solo trip to Walmart.

"Please, Sly. It's practically a rite of passage." I'd begged.

Eventually, Sly caved, probably because she wanted some butter pecan ice cream. The storm ended as abruptly as it started, so the drive was uneventful. Walmart was pretty quiet, too, as I grabbed Sly's ice cream and a jumbo-sized piece of poster board.

My presentation on the minerals of Montana isn't due for two more weeks. Still, I needed to justify the trip somehow. Besides, now that I have the poster board, maybe I'll get the project done early. Yeah, that won't happen.

On the drive home, I took a different route than usual, and what a surprise it brought me right by the construction site. Who am I kidding? My detour wouldn't surprise anyone who knows me.

Now, here I am, stumbling around in the dark, more frustrated by the minute. My dream nags me. I'm not sure why, but I think it's connected to this place.

I keep muttering the phrase from the song, "built his house upon the sand." I clang into a loose metal pipe that clangs into other metal objects, and the echo reverberates through the empty building.

"Yikes. Clean up on aisle three." I feel guilty for making a mess, but even I recognize this is a dangerous place. I need to leave. Walking back toward Sly's Honda, I'm reaching to open the car door when I see the flash of headlights. A car pulls into the long driveway.

Perfect. It's most likely Nick, out on patrol. He'll find me trespassing and take me home to Sly. I'll probably never see the inside of a Walmart again. And forget driving to Target in Missoula.

I move away from Sly's car, thankful that I didn't open the door. The interior light would shine like a beacon. I wait in the shadows, relieved there is no lightbar on the vehicle. Not Nick, then.

My relief changes to terror when the car stops, and Robert Sinclair steps out. In the brief second that I see his face, I can tell he isn't happy. I press back against the wall, thankful that it keeps me hidden from sight. A moment later, I hear gravel crunch as another vehicle, this time a truck, pulls up beside Robert's car.

The driver gets out and calls, "Evening, Mr. Sinclair."

Robert grunts and replies, "Inside."

Such a charmer. The two men walk around some exposed beams and into the building.

A few years ago, Mamma painted a sign that hangs over our kitchen door. It says, *Make good choices*. She said she wanted us to see it every day as we left the house. 'A gentle reminder,' she said. I didn't go through the kitchen door today. I'm not sure if it would've made a difference, but I make a choice. I really hope it's a good one.

I follow Robert and Mr. Pickup into the building. Only one side is completed, which should mean I can see by the moonlight. But as I discovered in my trip through the building earlier, there is no moonlight.

A flashlight comes on, and Robert orders, "Turn that thing off!" The flashlight goes out, but at least that brief moment gives me an idea where they are standing.

I carefully edge closer, praying I don't knock over any more clangy building supplies. I must move faster than I thought because the next time Robert speaks, he's standing a few feet from me. I stop and hold my breath.

"The buckets of sand are over here." Robert points to a corner of the building.

At the word *sand,* the tiny hairs on my neck stand up and wave. With barely a thought for why I'm doing it, I take out my phone. Turning my back to block any light, I find the record icon and tap it. The little red light blinks, showing that it's recording what they say. I tiptoe in the direction where Robert and Mr. Pickup were heading. I need to be close to make sure I get a good recording.

Robert removes a key from his pocket and unlocks a door to what appears to be a storage area. When they're standing inside the room, Robert lets Mr. Pickup turn on his flashlight. I creep closer, positioning my phone for the recording while still shielding the light.

"I still don't get the problem," Mr. Pickup grouches. "You knew this mixture has pyrite in it. That's why the boss gave you such a great deal. Concrete is concrete. You mix it with water, make cement, and you're good to go."

"And that was the plan," says Robert slowly, like he's talking to a particularly dense child. "But a nosey little girl started snooping around, and now it's got to go."

When he says, 'nosey little girl,' I wonder if he has spotted me. Then, I realize he's talking about Sly taking pictures for her class.

As I'm processing this information, I get a text from Sly.

Where are you? And where is my butter pecan ice cream?

I like variety, so I change the tones on my phone pretty often. Just this morning, I switched my text notification from Ding, one of the softer tones, to something a little ... louder.

Another not-so-good-decision.

The airhorn shatters the silence, and then a lot of things

happen at once. I drop my phone, and Robert wheels around to face me.

"I don't get paid enough for this." Mr. Pickup runs out the door.

Leaving me alone with Robert Sinclair. And his gun.

21

Sunday, September 23
7:45 p.m.

"FBI! Freeze!"

Now I understand the phrase, *My blood ran cold*. No one has to tell me to freeze. I have a crazy mental picture of an FBI agent running up to tag me, so I can unfreeze. That doesn't happen.

Sudden lights blaze, and several men and women surround us, guns drawn, pointed straight at Robert Sinclair. At least I hope they're all pointed at him. I glance around, looking for that cute Dr. Spencer Reid from the TV show, *Criminal Minds*. Then, I realize this is real life, those are real guns, and I'm in real trouble.

As if to emphasize that thought, Robert starts to raise his gun.

"Don't do it, Robert," a growly voice says. Nick.

"Mr. Sinclair." A second growly voice.

One I don't recognize. I have another hysterical thought— are all officers of the law required to take a growly voice class? I'll ask Nick later.

"Robert Sinclair, you are under arrest for conspiracy to

commit fraud. Don't add attempted murder to your crimes," Unknown Growly Voice says.

For a moment, everyone seems to hold their breath as we watch the wheels turn in Robert's mind. Then, he slowly lowers the gun, and quick as lightning, an agent rushes forward to take it away. Within seconds, several other men and women surround Robert. They wear dark jackets with FBI printed out in bright letters on the back.

Nick and Sheriff Richards come to stand beside me, and one of the FBI agents walks toward us.

"Ms. Thomas." It takes me a minute to understand he's talking to me.

"Yes, sir," I squeak.

"Sheriff Richards and Deputy McBride will drive you to the Sheriff's station. We'll talk to you there." Mr. FBI walks away.

I turn to Nick. "Am I in trouble?" I ask quietly.

"Not the legal kind," is all he says. Then Nick reaches out to give me a hard hug. "Jess, you have no idea how scared I was when Robert pointed that gun at you. It's a miracle you didn't get hurt or even killed."

I tremble as the reality sets in. "I know," I whisper. "I think God protected me—again. How did you figure out what was happening?"

We all walk toward the squad car.

"The FBI has been watching Robert Sinclair ever since they executed the search warrant for the lumber the other day." Sheriff Richards answers my question. "They also recovered more pictures that Robert deleted from Sly's SD card. One photo showed a bucket of concrete mixture their experts identified as substandard. That particular kind has something in it that makes the concrete crumble after a brief time."

"Pyrite," I offer.

The Sheriff gives me a startled look.

I hold up my phone. "I recorded what Robert said about the concrete."

Sheriff Richards starts to look impressed but resists. He probably doesn't want to encourage me. "Yes, he deliberately bought cheap, substandard materials, and he pocketed the extra profit. The FBI suspected Robert would try to destroy the evidence, so when they saw him come in here tonight, they followed him. You, however, were a surprise." The Sheriff stares hard at me.

I squirm slightly. Nick opens the rear door of the squad car and helps me in. For a second, I wonder if I just experienced my first perp walk. No handcuffs. That has to be a good sign.

I ride to the station with Sheriff Richards. Nick drives Sly's Honda to our house and picks her up. No one can interview me until Sly arrives because she's my guardian.

My conversation with the FBI agents is short but not so sweet. While they're grateful for the evidence I've given them, they also point out how reckless I was.

Sly sits beside me the whole time, alternately squeezing my hand and kicking my ankle. I'm not sure if she's upset because I almost got shot or because the butter pecan ice cream melted all over the back seat of her car. Probably both.

I try focusing on what the FBI agents are saying. I do. But I'm distracted by their badges that read Special Agent. I overhear acronyms like CODIS and AFIS, and I feel a little shimmer under my skin. The agents and their work fascinate me. There's something I can't explain happening inside of me. It's nearly a longing. I'll examine that feeling in-depth. Later.

Sunday, September 23
10:00 p.m.

COLE, Grace, and Maggie are waiting on the porch swing when Sly and I pull into the driveway. Mr. and Mrs. McBride's Mazda sits next to the basketball hoop, and Nick parks the squad car beside it.

"Hey," I say with false enthusiasm as we climb the steps. "Looks like we're having a party. It's too bad we don't have any ice cream."

Sly glares at me. "Too soon," is all she says as she leads Nick into the house.

Maggie squeals and races across the porch to hug me. "I was so scared. I thought you got arrested, too, and I wouldn't have any family left to live with me."

I look down at her tear covered face. "You're leaking," I tease, trying to make her smile.

But it doesn't work. She leaks harder.

"Magpie." I bend down, looking into her eyes. "Everything's okay now. Sly and I are not going anywhere, I promise."

"You can't promise," Maggie says in a very solemn voice, and my heart hurts for her.

"You're right, Maggie," I say. "I wish I could promise nothing bad will ever happen again, but I can't. But I do promise this— we can always trust God to help us, no matter what happens. He says so, and God is the only one who always keeps his promises. Always."

Maggie studies me for a moment, then nods her head. "Yes," she says. "I do believe *Him*."

She gives me another hug, then turns to run up the steps.

Grace and Cole wait until Maggie disappears before they speak. It's like they've rehearsed or something.

Grace: "What were you thinking?"

Cole: "She wasn't."

Grace: "Why did you go there alone?"

Cole: "Because she acts first and thinks later."

Grace puts her hands on her hips, a move I've seen when she's trying to make the Ellison twins behave.

"Well, don't you have anything to say?" she asks.

Torn between annoyance and amusement, I shrug. "I didn't know it was my turn."

She appears confused for a minute, shakes her head, and gives me a quick hug. "Please tell me you've retired from detective work."

I decide this might not be the best time to discuss my growing interest in the FBI. That can wait. I squeeze her back. "I'm safe now."

She studies me, and I'm pretty sure I haven't fooled her.

But eventually, she steps back. "I'll leave you two to talk."

Then Cole and I are alone. He takes my hand and leads me to sit beside him on the porch swing. For several minutes we don't say a word—we simply sit there holding hands, staring straight ahead, swinging.

"Are you mad at me?" I finally ask.

"Yes."

I turn toward him, a little surprised at the prompt answer. He doesn't seem angry, though. He just looks sad.

"Cole."

He lets go of my hand and turns to face me. "Let me get this out, Jess."

My heart drops. He sounds so serious.

"I care about you. A lot. I think, or thought, I guess, that you care about me."

I open my mouth to say something.

But Cole shakes his head to stop me. "After the accident with Mark, I asked you to trust me, remember?"

A lump forms in my throat as I nod. I've never seen Cole look like this. So distant.

"After you jumped in my truck and rode to Robert's house, I asked you again to trust me. I wanted you to tell me what you were thinking and not go off on your own. I asked you to be safe." Cole's dark gray eyes focus on mine.

I want to look away but can't.

"Jess, good relationships need trust. I wasn't asking you not to be who you are. I *like* who you are. But I want you to trust me and be honest with me. If you told me you wanted to check out the construction site again, I would have gone with you.

"I wouldn't have liked it, and I might have tried to talk you out of the idea, but at least we would have been communicating. Instead, you do your own thing. Again. And that makes me not trust you."

Tears roll down my cheeks, and I angrily brush them away. How can Cole say he doesn't trust me?

"Jess, I want a relationship with you. But maybe we aren't ready yet. We need to go back to being just friends, for now. We need time to rebuild what we've lost." Then he stops the swing, stands up, and walks away.

I stare straight ahead, struggling not to throw myself down on the swing and sob for a few years. Tonight was terrifying, even if I tried to make jokes in front of everyone else. I counted on Cole to comfort and reassure me. Instead, he left me. Alone.

A moment later, the front door opens, and Grace steps out. "Did Cole leave already?"

"Yes," I whisper. "Cole is gone."

My tone must have alerted her because Grace joins me on the swing. "Jess." She gently touches my arm.

Without a word, I turn and lay my head on my best friend's shoulder. Then I sob.

22

Tuesday, September 25
7:00 p.m.

"H appy birthday, Maggie! Where's the birthday girl?" Mr. and Mrs. McBride's greetings blend together.

"Come in." Sly welcomes them inside.

My hands tremble a little as I set the dining room table with pink and turquoise plastic plates. A large cake proclaiming *Happy Birthday Maggie* sits in a place of honor on the table.

Grace enters from the kitchen carrying napkins and cups matching the plates. Sensing my mood, she doesn't say anything but places them down and returns to the kitchen for the ice cream.

Brushing an annoying tear from my eye, I concentrate, lining the birthday decorations in precise order. At least I can do that right, I think. Then I'm disgusted by my own self-pity.

"Get over it, Jess," I scold myself. "Today isn't about you."

As the laughing guests approach the dining room, I straighten my shoulders, practicing a fake smile. The mirror hanging above Grandma Thomas's antique buffet reflects my attempt. It looks like I'm baring my teeth to take a bite out of someone. I unclench my jaw and try again. Better.

Mr. and Mrs. McBride enter the room, followed by a grinning Maggie. Sly and Nick stand in the doorway, holding hands. We were all thrilled when Robert Sinclair confessed to lying about Sly's supposed theft from his company.

When the FBI asked Robert why he didn't destroy the camera, he shrugged and said he'd stashed it in the closet, planning to toss it later. He hadn't expected a 16-year-old girl to break into his office. Robert even had the nerve to ask the FBI to charge me. Fortunately, they declined.

They dropped all charges against Sly, although she still doesn't have a job. But for now, we're thankful God gave us justice.

"Happy birthday, Magpie." I plant a quick kiss on the top of her head.

Maggie laughs. "That's the tenth time you've said that today."

"It can't be said enough," I answer. "C'mon, let's eat!"

"We're waiting for Rachel," Maggie says. "Her mom is dropping her off in a minute."

Rachel and Maggie have been besties since the first day of kindergarten when Maggie saved Rachel from accidentally walking into the boy's bathroom instead of the girls. Considering stuff like that can follow a kid for the rest of their school days, Rachel is devoted to Maggie.

The front door opens with its usual squeak, and Maggie races out of the room to greet her friend.

But the "Happy Birthday" greeting from the foyer is in a much deeper voice than Rachel's.

Maggie reappears, tugging Cole behind her. "See, Jess?" Maggie says with little sister innocence. "Cole *did* come."

My face flushes, and I turn toward the kitchen, calling over my shoulder, "That's nice. I'll get the ice for the drinks." I race into the kitchen, going straight to the freezer to pull out an oversized bag of ice. Then I reach into the cabinet for an equally oversized bowl.

"Here, let me help you," Cole says from behind.

Of course, I drop the ice. It lands on my toe with a painful thump. I lean down to pick it up just as Cole does, and we crack our heads together.

"Ouch." I stand up, glaring at Cole while I rub my forehead. "You have a hard head," I accuse.

Cole raises an eyebrow. "So, do you," he says.

I'm pretty sure he isn't talking about our head-on collision. He reaches above my head, grabbing the bowl from the cupboard and placing it on the counter. Then he takes the bag from my shaking hands and pours the ice into the container. I reach for the bowl.

But Cole blocks me. "Jess, can we talk?"

"I'm pretty sure we already did that," I say and try to reach around him for the ice bowl.

He steps in front of me again. "I'm sorry. I was mad."

"Was?" I ask. "As in, you're not mad anymore?"

Cole shrugs. "I'm still a little mad," he admits. "But I realized that if I expect you to trust me, I need to be trustworthy."

I open my mouth to respond.

"Wait." Cole shakes his head. "I practiced this all the way over here, so don't distract me." He steps closer and reaches for my hands. "Jess, you've been through a lot in the last year. More than anyone should have to deal with. You lost your parents and nearly had your sister taken out of your life. Honestly, I'm a little in awe of how well you've kept it together."

Tears sting my eyes at his unexpected words of praise.

"You scared me." Cole reaches up and gently brushes away one of the tears. "And to tell the truth, I was scared at how scared I was, if that makes any sense. I care about you, more than I ever knew, and the thought of you getting hurt ..." Cole's voice cracks a little.

I look at him. Really look at him. His gray eyes tell me even better than his words that he's scared of losing me—not only relationally, but forever.

"I'm so sorry." I reach up to touch his cheek, which is a little rough with whiskers. I like whiskers.

Cole turns his head, placing his lips against my palm, and I step closer. He gathers me in his arms and holds me tight, then pulls back to look at me.

"Let's start over," he says.

I nod.

This time the kiss is more intense than the night of Homecoming. When Cole raises his head to look at me, he takes a shuddering breath and leans down again. I close my eyes, preparing for more kissing, and then open them when he misses my lips and kisses my forehead.

"We should get back," he says.

I nod. "Yes, we should." We don't move.

Cole pulls me closer again, and I lay my cheek against his chest, snuggling into his green flannel shirt. He smells good—kind of piney like the forest. I like piney.

A few seconds pass, and Cole chuckles. "Girl, we are going to have such adventures."

I have a strange feeling that he is promising a lifetime of adventures. I decide I like adventures.

We walk into the dining room, and Cole places the ice bowl on the table, next to the soft drinks.

"Bro, the ice is melted," Nick observes.

Cole grins. "Sure is."

AFTER THE PARTY, Maggie and Rachel race outside to play hide and seek with Roxie. I know from experience that the road through the pre-teen years is not a straight line. One day you're learning to walk in heels, and the next, you're curled up on the couch with your favorite ratty blanket, watching cartoon reruns.

Sly enters the kitchen, where I'm attempting to put plastic wrap over the cake. It's beyond me why we can put a man on the moon, but no one can make plastic wrap that doesn't wad up in long, annoying strips.

"So," Sly says, nudging me with her hip.

I nudge her back. "So."

"All good?" she asks.

"Better than," I say.

Sly and I have our own language.

She nods and says, "Good talk," then leaves the room.

Grace comes in, carrying the paper plates, used napkins, and empty plastic cups. She dumps them all in the trash can, then walks to the sink. As she washes and dries her hands, she says, "Well, my work here is done."

I point to the cake, covered in long, tangled wads of saran wrap. "Mine, too."

The song from Beauty and the Beast, "Be our Guest," plays, and I nod at Grace's black quilted vest. "Your clothes are ringing."

Grace pulls out her phone, then says, "Kellen asked if you and Cole want to go see a movie with us?"

"I think so," I say, unsure.

Cole walks into the room, holding his phone. "Jess, should we go with Grace and Kellen to a movie?"

We. Nodding my agreement to the plan, I decide I *really* like the word we.

As we enter the living room, I hear Sly's ringtone, and I panic, thinking Kellen is inviting Nick and Sly, too. Awkward. But from Sly's response, I know the call isn't from Kellen.

"Yes, of course, I'll tell them, and we'll all be praying." Sly turns off her phone. "That was Nick. While you were in the kitchen, he was called into work because of an accident. Apparently, Mark Crowley and some of his buddies combined drinking while riding their ATVs. Mark was going too fast and hit a log. He flipped over the handlebars and landed on some rocks. Nick says it's serious."

My knees buckle, and I abruptly sit down on the arm of the sofa. Cole comes to stand beside me.

Mr. McBride stands. "Let's pray, right now. Father, please protect the life of this young man, Mark. Guide the doctors as they treat him for his injuries. Give his family comfort and peace, and most of all, draw Mark's heart to You. In Jesus' name we pray, amen."

A chorus of "amens" sounds around the room.

All the emotions I've felt concerning Mark roil through me: anger, hurt, and unforgiveness. But now they're replaced with deep sadness as I consider that Mark might face eternity—without Jesus.

23

Saturday, September 29
7:00 p.m.

"Y ou don't have to do this, Jess," Cole says again.

We walk through the glass doors of the St. James Hospital, and I rub my clammy hands along the sides of my jeans, considering his words. Today, we finally saw the movie with Grace and Kellen, which we'd canceled the night of Maggie's party.

After the movie, we headed to my house for pizzas and board games. But we'd just arrived home when Cole received a surprising text from Mark, asking Cole to visit him in the hospital.

My heart raced when Cole told me where he was going. For the past several days, I've struggled with whether I should tell Cole that Mark took me to Bannack. Mark was in a coma for a full day after the accident, and we hadn't known if he'd ever wake up. I couldn't allow myself to say anything bad about him, even the truth.

When we told Sly we were going to St. James Hospital, she hugged me and whispered, "I'll be praying for you."

I saw those same emotions visible on Grace and Kellen's faces, and I know it's not because of Mark.

Ten months ago, I'd raced through these doors with my sisters, terrified by the news of our parent's accident. But, by the time we arrived in the ER, they were already gone. I haven't been to this hospital since, and it's more difficult than I imagined. Now, the sounds, smells, and urgent concern on the faces of the visitors bring back that night in vivid color.

"Hey." Cole stops walking and draws me into an alcove off the reception area. "Jess, I told you I can visit Mark on my own. You don't need to put yourself through this."

"I have to go," I say. "I need to apologize to Mark."

Cole's eyebrows shoot up, and he starts to say something.

I raise my hand to stop him. "The fact is, crashing into that tree is as much my fault as Mark's. I wanted to see the construction site. If I hadn't gone with him, he wouldn't have been on that road. And I should have visited him after our accident and talked to him." My voice shakes. "Mark could have died this time."

"The fact is," Cole repeats my words, "Mark is in the hospital because he was drinking and drove his ATV at a dangerous speed. That's not on you." Cole takes a deep breath. "Look, why don't you sit in the waiting room and—"

"I need to do this." I cut him off with such a firm shake of my head, my hair swirls around my face.

He studies me for a minute. "Okay."

We turn toward the elevator at the end of the corridor, and Cole punches the button. When the door slides open, we get on. As the door closes, I breathe deeper. Maybe I could pretend we're in a mall or office building and not a hospital. Not *this* hospital.

We find Mark's room on the third floor, and Cole knocks on the half-open door. Mark calls, "Come in," and as we enter, I get my first look at his injuries. A white plaster cast engulfs his broken left leg. It hangs suspended from a harness attached to pulleys. Dark bruises mottle his face and arms, and there's a gauze bandage wrapped around the top of his head.

But that isn't the only change. All his arrogance and attitude are gone, and there is nothing left of the old Mark sneer. In fact, he looks sad and a little scared.

"Thank you for coming," he says as we approach the bed.

Cole clears his throat, and I can tell Mark's condition is also affecting him. "How are you?"

Mark gives a wry chuckle. "I've been better." He nods at two chairs placed near the bed. "Why don't you sit down? I'll try to make this quick."

We silently settle onto the hard, plastic seats.

"Jess, please forgive me for what I did," Mark says, "I took a crazy risk with your life, and I'm very sorry."

A lump forms in my throat, and it feels like all the anger I had is draining away. Mark looks so young and broken. I reach over and gently touch his arm. "I forgive you, Mark. Will you forgive me?"

He seems surprised and shakes his head, "No. You have nothing to apologize for."

"I do," I say. "If I hadn't accepted your invitation, our accident wouldn't have happened. I was using you to get what I wanted, which was a ride to the Emerson Construction Site."

Mark frowns.

"That's probably a story for another time," Cole says.

I nod and continue, "The point is, I'm as much to blame as you. And I should have come to see you then, instead of waiting until you were nearly killed this time." I lose the battle with my tears and let them fall.

Cole reaches over and squeezes my hand.

Mark looks thoughtful. "Let's divide it up this way. You can accept 5 percent of the responsibility, and I'll take 95 percent." He lifts his right hand. "I broke my little finger in that accident," he says. "That's all on you."

I see a glint of humor in his eyes, and I'm startled into a chuckle.

Brushing my palms across my face, I wipe away the tears. "Mark," I say solemnly, "I'm sorry I broke your little finger."

"Forgiven." Then his eyes are sad again. "I could have killed you, Jess."

Cole shifts in his chair and makes a deep noise that sounds like a growl. I look at him, startled, but Mark nods as if he agrees with the sentiment.

"When I woke up after this last accident, I realized something has to change, or I may never make it to 18. I need to tell the truth, to you and especially to myself." Mark looks directly at Cole. "I took Jess up to Bannack to get back at you. I thought you told Nick I'd been drinking."

The words come out in a rush. It's like he's afraid if he doesn't spit them out now, they might never come.

The room remains silent as Mark and I watch Cole, waiting for his reaction. Then Cole stands so abruptly his plastic chair tips over and clangs to the floor. Not even bothering to pick it up, he walks to the window. Turning his back, he stares at the scattered lights of the city.

"Why?"

I assume Cole's question is for Mark, so I'm surprised when he turns and looks straight at me. Hurt is clear in his eyes.

"Why didn't you tell me, Jess? I thought you'd driven to Dillon. Why didn't you tell me Mark took you to Bannack?"

I barely glance in Cole's eyes before I have to look away. My heart pounds as I consider how to explain my silence.

"I think she was protecting me," Mark says.

Cole crosses the room in a flash. "Did you hurt her, Mark?"

I'd never heard Cole use that tone before.

"No!" Mark and I speak at the same time.

I hurry to touch Cole's arm. "Please, Cole. Come and sit down and let him tell you everything."

He glares at Mark for another moment, then reluctantly pulls his chair upright and sits, crossing his arms.

"Talk," he demands.

It impresses me that Mark doesn't frantically push the button to call the nurse. Or maybe S.W.A.T.

Instead, he returns Cole's direct look and says, "I was furious when Nick arrested me for drinking, and I figured you were the one who told him."

Cole stirs.

"I know now it wasn't you." Mark continues. "I'd broken up with Tabitha. She was mad, so she made an anonymous call to Nick. She visited me yesterday and told me what she'd done." Mark shifts in the bed.

He must be so uncomfortable, lying in that position for days.

"I decided the best way to pay you back was to hurt Jess—or at least her reputation. I told my buddies Jess asked me to drive her to Bannack, and I let them fill in the blanks about why."

Cole growls again. What is he, part wolf?

"I never planned to touch her or hurt her," Mark hurries to say, "I promise. I may be a jerk, but I'm not completely evil." Mark looks away and swallows. When he speaks again, his voice is husky. "Everyone likes and respects you, Cole. Honestly, I think I hated you for that. Turns out, I actually hated me."

He looks from Cole to me. "Please, listen, both of you. I am sorry for everything I did to you. I know it's unforgivable, but I'll do anything you ask to make it up to you. I'm not sure where to start."

"It's not unforgivable," I whisper.

Cole leans forward, his elbows on his knees. He stares at the floor, obviously processing Mark's confession.

Finally, he looks up. "Mark, Jess and I are both Christians, and we know we have to forgive you if we want Jesus to forgive us. It's not an easy thing to do, but we are making a conscious decision to forgive. That doesn't mean our emotions are always there at first, but when we forgive, our emotions change, too."

I move to stand by Mark's bedside. "You don't owe us anything, Mark. I'm pretty sure you've already realized God protected us both that night like He protected you in the ATV accident. God has a reason for your life to continue. Maybe you should ask Him what to do next."

Mark gives a wry smile. "It's funny you should mention that. Your pastors both stopped by yesterday to introduce themselves and see how I was doing. We had a good talk, and Pastor Jeff plans to stop in again tomorrow. I have a lot of questions for him."

"Good." Cole nods and stands up. "He's a great guy, and you can trust him." He reaches out to shake Mark's good hand. "Let's start over," he says. "Mark, my name is Cole McBride, and this is Jess Thomas. She's my girlfriend."

Mark gives Cole's hand an enthusiastic shake and grins. "'Bout time."

24

Sunday, September 30
6:30 p.m.

"Yes, sir, that sounds wonderful. I appreciate the opportunity. Yes, I'll see you at 9:00 a.m. tomorrow morning." Sly ends the call and turns to face us.

After Mark's text last night, we rescheduled our game night. Now our friends sit around the dining room table: Cole, Nick, Kellen, Grace, Maggie, and even Mr. and Mrs. McBride.

Sly beams. "That was Mr. Anderson, the editor of *The Voice of Justice*. He offered me a job as a photographer for the newspaper. I'll also do some office admin jobs at first, but eventually, it can grow into a full-time position.

"Mr. Anderson was writing the story about Robert Sinclair tonight, and he was impressed by my photography skills when he saw the pictures I took. He also said the job comes with a tuition grant for my online photography classes." Sly's voice cracks a little.

Nick is right there to hug her. "That's amazing, Sly. You're a talented photographer, and the *Voice* is a respected newspaper. You'll be great."

We all gather around Sly, laughing and maybe even crying a little.

Mrs. McBride touches my arm. "Jessica, remember when we discussed how God can take a bad situation and turn it to good?"

I nod, barely able to talk. "Yes," I whisper. I think of all the frightening events of the past month, and in my heart, I hear Mamma's confident words, '*But God.*' I turn to give Mrs. McBride a tight hug, repeating those words with my own confidence, "But God."

There's a lot of laughter as we raid the kitchen for snacks and drinks. Mrs. McBride brought over her delicious *queso* with chips. It sits on Mamma's cherry buffet, alongside snack mix, veggies and dip, and the no-bake cookies Sly and Maggie made that afternoon. We're set for a night of gaming.

There are so many of us, I realize we won't have enough play money. I offer to raid other games for whatever currency I can find. Running up to my room, I root through my closet, pulling out games, puzzles, and even Mrs. Flurry, my old stuffed penguin. I take a minute to hug her, sneeze from the dust, and keep looking.

Pulling out several old backpacks, I grab the bag I took with me the night I found Sly's camera in Robert's office. As I toss it behind me, a manila file folder slides from the pocket and onto the floor.

I study it for a minute in confusion, then remember I'd found this folder in Robert's office. I'd grabbed it because our last name was on it. But, with all the excitement of finding the camera and the pictures, I'd completely forgotten about the files.

For a minute, I consider stuffing the folder back in the bag and burying it deep in my closet. For some reason, my heart is pounding, and my breath comes faster. Reaching down, I pick it up and read.

Scanning the contents, I see the names Robert Sinclair and Anthony Avery. And at the very bottom of the page is a signature I recognize well. Brian Thomas. Next to Daddy's signature is a date. Dizziness swamps me as I realize Daddy signed this report the day before my parents' accident.

I sit on my bedroom floor for several minutes, attempting to comprehend what I've just read and interpret what it might mean.

In the background, I hear the laughter of my family and friends. Mr. and Mrs. McBride, who are becoming very important in our lives. Sly and Nick. I love seeing them together and watching their love deepen. Maggie, who is healing from the trauma of loss. Grace, my dearest friend, and Kellen, who is smoothly melding into our group.

And Cole. My throat tightens, and my eyes burn as I remember Cole's words a few days earlier. "*Girl, we are going to have such an adventure.*"

"Hey, Jess," Cole calls from the bottom of the steps. "Are you printing the money up there?"

A few days ago, Cole asked me to trust him and not attempt to fix everything on my own. I squeeze my eyes closed, wishing I could go back in time a few minutes. Back before I came in here and found this file. But that's a fantasy. This is as real as it gets.

This month has been so hard. We need some time to process everything that's happened. The laughter drifts up again, and my heart aches. My sisters need a few days of peace. Maggie's nightmares have almost stopped. Sly is falling in love with Nick. Tomorrow, she'll start to live her dream of being a photojournalist.

I'll keep this secret for a little while. But one thing I've learned this past month is that I can trust God in this next challenge. I breathe the prayer, 'Please help us, God,' and somehow, I trust He will.

Decision made, I push the file deep into the bottom of the backpack. Then I stuff it under my old Disney Princess sleeping bag, far back in the corner of my closet. Digging around, I spot a bag of play money, grab it, then head for the door.

A moment later, I walk into the dining room, fanning the

wad of bills in my hand. I look into the faces of the people I love
so much.

"Ok, family," I say. "Let's play this game called Life."

ABOUT DEBBI MIGIT

Award-winning author and speaker Debbi Migit lives in central Illinois, surrounded by pumpkin patches and cornfields. Her first book, Child of Promise, is the true love story of a family formed through adoption. After ten years of infertility, Debbi and her husband Phil were just months from adopting when God said, "Not this way." Child of Promise is the story of audacious faith resulting in multiple miracles. It encourages readers to remember their own promises and believe again.

She has won multiple awards and contests, writing stories that are filled with faith and hope. She loves to share personal anecdotes about God's faithfulness, infusing her talks with authenticity and humor. Debbi and Phil are the adoptive parents of Alex (31), Ethan (20), and Kate (19). The God-ordained spacing of their children offered the unique opportunity to parent a teen and two toddlers–at the same time. This is the season Debbi fondly calls the TNT years!

Debbi's hobbies include reading, writing, and avoiding arithmetic. Her favorite color is turquoise, and she collects Trixie Belden books and typewriters. If playing Candy Crush was a paying gig, she would be rich.

Debbi's new romance/suspense series begins with September Shadows and is set in Montana. After the mysterious death of their parents, three young sisters are determined to stay together and make a new life for themselves. This new life includes faith-testing danger, adventure, and romance.

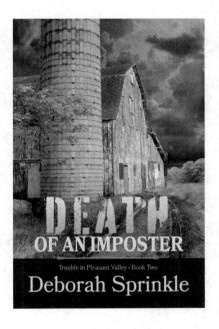

Death of an Imposter

Trouble in Pleasant Valley

Book Two

Rookie detective Bernadette Santos has her first murder case. Will her desire for justice end up breaking her heart? Or worse —get her killed!

Her first week on the job and rookie detective Bernadette Santos has been given the murder of a prominent citizen to solve. But when her victim turns out to be an imposter, her straight forward case takes a nasty turn. One that involves the attractive Dr. Daniel O'Leary, a visitor to Pleasant Valley and a man harboring secrets.

When Dr. O'Leary becomes a target of violence himself, Detective Santos has two mysteries to unravel. Are they related? And how far can she trust the good doctor? Her heart tugs her one way while her mind pulls her another. She must discover the solutions before it's too late!

Books Afloat
Columbia River Undercurrents
Book One

Blaming herself for her childhood role in the Oklahoma farm truck accident that cost her grandfather's life, Anne Mettles is determined to make her life count. She wants to do it all–captain her library boat and resist Japanese attacks to keep America safe. But failing her pilot's exam requires her to bring others onboard.

Will she go it alone? Or will she team with the unlikely but (mostly) lovable characters? One is a saboteur, one an unlikely hero, and one, she discovers, is the man of her dreams.

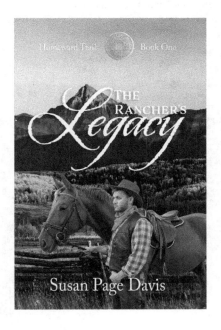

The Rancher's Legacy

Homeward Trails

Book One - Coming February 23, 2021

Available for pre-order now!

Matthew Anderson and his father try to help neighbor Bill Maxwell when his ranch is attacked. On the day his daughter Rachel is to return from school back East, outlaws target the Maxwell ranch. After Rachel's world is shattered, she won't even consider the plan her father and Matt's cooked up—to see their two children marry and combine the ranches.

Meanwhile in Maine, sea captain's widow Edith Rose hires a private investigator to locate her three missing grandchildren. The children were abandoned by their father nearly twenty years ago. They've been adopted into very different families, and they're scattered across the country. Can investigator Ryland Atkins find them all while the elderly woman still lives? His first attempt is to find the boy now called Matthew Anderson. Can Ryland survive his trip into the wild Colorado Territory and find Matt before the outlaws finish destroying a legacy?

Scrivenings
PRESS
Quench your thirst for story.
www.ScriveningsPress.com

Stay up-to-date on your favorite books and authors with our free e-newsletters.

ScriveningsPress.com

CPSIA information can be obtained
at www.ICGtesting.com
Printed in the USA
LVHW050412010221
677984LV00017B/998

9 781649 170866